D0328530

The Miracle of Anna: An Awakened Child

Book One

The Miracle of Anna:
An Awakened Child

Book One

John Nelson

Winchester, UK
Washington, USA

First published by Roundfire Books, 2019
Roundfire Books is an imprint of John Hunt Publishing Ltd., No. 3 East St., Alresford,
Hampshire SO24 9EE, UK
office1@jhpbooks.net
www.johnhuntpublishing.com
www.roundfire-books.com

For distributor details and how to order please visit the 'Ordering' section on our website.

Text copyright: John Nelson 2018

ISBN: 978 1 78535 929 3
978 1 78535 930 9 (ebook)
Library of Congress Control Number: 2017962585

All rights reserved. Except for brief quotations in critical articles or reviews, no part of this book
may be reproduced in any manner without prior written permission from the publishers.

The rights of John Nelson as author have been asserted in accordance with the Copyright, Designs
and Patents Act 1988.

A CIP catalogue record for this book is available from the British Library.

Design: Stuart Davies

Printed and bound by CPI Group (UK) Ltd, Croydon, CR0 4YY, UK

We operate a distinctive and ethical publishing philosophy in
all areas of our business, from our global network of authors to
production and worldwide distribution.

9454040020

To Sri Anandamayi Ma, whose early life story was the inspiration for this novel.

By John Nelson

Starborn

Transformations

Matrix of the Gods

The Magic Mirror

I, Human

A Guide to Energetic Healing

"What I am, I have been from my infancy."
—Anandamayi Ma

Chapter 1

When asked years later about the pregnancy and birth of her daughter Anna by dreamy inquirers expecting to hear sacred tales with celestial harbingers, Maggie would laugh and irreverently tell them, "It wasn't an immaculate conception, for sure," although her guru did foretell Anna's birth and sanctity. Actually, if her unborn baby's ability to talk to her was a sign of her elevated spiritual status, there was also that to consider. So they would smile indulgently at Maggie and glance at each other with doubtful looks to remind themselves that holy water can be carried by tainted vessels.

Such zealots were rarely in tune with her daughter's presence as a child and later in life, for Anna was the most "present" and least starry-eyed person she had ever known, and Maggie had met a few on her own spiritual journey. This may seem surprising given the mystical trance states that Anna so readily came to occupy and which first drew attention to her as an awakened child. To illustrate this point, Maggie loved to tell the story of coming upon her two-year-old daughter in a trance state and being mesmerized by the child's saintly aura, only to have Anna tell Maggie, with her eyes still closed and her trance undisturbed, "Mama, water boiling."

Maggie had been unprepared for the arrival of any child, not least one with Anna's spiritual lineage. She had been visiting her guru Ma hi' Ma's ashram in Northern California for the Hindu *Maha Shivaratri* festival in mid-March, or the great night of Lord Shiva. There she met Thomas, a Kundalini Yoga teacher from Seattle. He was tall and thin with a mop of curly brown hair and as limber and sexy as a feline. Maggie was immediately attracted to him. She attended one of his classes, and when Thomas's delicate hands touched her to correct a posture, Maggie felt surges of energy running up and down her body. Lithe and below average height, she was light-haired with green eyes and a heart-shaped pixie face, and drew a lot of male attention. While some teachers are known to activate the kundalini energy in their students, Thomas was not that advanced of a practitioner. This was due more to Maggie's sexual response than to any transference of *Shakti*. She had been celibate for a while from a lack of opportunity and disposition but recognized the stimulated energy. The attraction was mutual as Thomas found the need to constantly adjust her postures that first session. Finally, one of the other female students petulantly told them to "get a room, will you?"

This stifled their budding relationship as they avoided each other for the rest of the week. It was a large ashram and there were many religious activities to keep them occupied and apart. But, as fate would have it, the following Saturday the two of them found themselves sitting across from each other in the wide meditation circle surrounding their guru during the early-evening satsang. They tried to focus on her discourse, but inevitably their eyes came to rest on each other, and Maggie became noticeably flushed by this eye exchange. That night a group of them headed over the mountain to Santa Rosa for dinner and spiritual discussion before their one-day fast. Thomas arranged to sit next to Maggie at the long dinner table, and they talked to each other exchanging personal histories and spiritual perspectives and rarely took part in the general discussion.

"Do you paint with oil on canvas?" Thomas asked at one point.

"I'm more into watercolors and depictions of mystical landscapes."

"A budding Turner?" he teased.

Maggie smiled. "A budding Langford."

Thomas laughed. "I like that. A woman claiming her power."

Maggie nodded her head in appreciation, but she had to cross her legs to manage the stirring energy. At the end of the night, it became obvious to all that Thomas and Maggie needed to spend more time together, so those who came with Thomas in his van stuffed themselves into the other van and drove back to the ashram. The two of them sat in the van's bucket seats in the parking lot talking until two o'clock in the morning, while Maggie waited for him to make the first move. Finally her alluring smiles drew the desired response; Thomas blew up an air mattress and they made love in the back of the van.

They used condoms the first two times, but that was all Thomas could scare up, and stores were closed at this hour. Knowing her monthly cycle, Maggie figured it was safe to continue; she just couldn't get enough of him, or was something else driving this coupling, she would soon wonder? They made love again, and the intensity of their sexual congress created a perceptible glow around them both. Finally, they fell asleep wrapped around each other on the air mattress with a blanket flung over them. Their tryst ended rather abruptly hours later when a cop pounded his fist on the side of the van and told them to move on. They hurriedly dressed and drove back to the ashram in time for morning prayers. At the convocation hall, they entered separately five minutes apart, and didn't seem to draw anybody's interest. But, at morning satsang, Ma hi' Ma was answering a young woman's inquiry when she abruptly stopped, scanned the room, and her eyes came to rest on Maggie. The intensity of that long stare did attract attention, and she soon found the assembly gawking at her. Was this the ashram's equivalent of *The Scarlet Letter*?

Ma hi' Ma smiled and closed her eyes, swaying in her customary ecstatic trance state, which lasted some thirty minutes and at least drew attention away from Maggie back to their guru. At noon prayers, one of those chosen to attend to Guru summoned Maggie to an audience with her. *Oh shit*, she thought. *Now I'm going to hear it.* She followed after Prema, a waiflike creature who seemed to walk on air, and once again all eyes were focused on her. Their guru lived in the main house, or the Palace as everyone called it—a converted plantation house with white Dorian columns, high ceilings and massive windows, all impeccably kept clean. The ceiling of the temple room had been converted into a dome shape with skylights, its pine wood floors covered with Persian rugs and embroidered pillows with Hindu art. Ma hi' Ma sat atop a small mountain of them and smiled at Maggie, who gingerly made her approach with hands in folded prayer mode and her head bowed. Her guru was a Westerner, actually from Boston and of Irish descent, and while she had lost her Southey accent, she still retained the direct manner of a street fighter.

"Sit down, child," she told her.

Guru looked around the room, and her attendants all stood and marched out, closing the high double doors behind them.

"You look tired," Guru said.

Maggie had never spoken directly to her and wasn't sure if she was meant to reply.

"Has the cat got your tongue?"

Maggie glanced up. "We went to dinner last night and I... stayed up late."

Her guru smiled knowingly. "Yes, very late." She paused. "Get some rest before tonight's meditation."

Maggie nodded.

"I have detected a spiritual presence around you, a soul that wishes to enter." She paused. "You are single, are you not?"

"Yes, Ma," Maggie replied, as she had heard others address their guru.

"This is a great soul and I would suggest that, if you are willing, to find a consort...if you haven't already," Ma said with a coy smile, "since I'm sure neither of us believes in immaculate conceptions."

"Yes, Ma." Maggie looked down. *So did Guru know of last night's indiscretion, and did she get pregnant by a man she hardly knew? And not just any baby, a great soul. Oh boy,* she thought, almost grinding her teeth.

Ma paused for a moment, closed her eyes, and then laughed to herself. "You will name her Anna, and we will see what will come of this most auspicious opening for you."

Maggie raised her eyes but did not speak, somewhat overwhelmed by the import of this directive.

"That will be all, child. We will be in touch, and if you have any needs, make us aware of them, and they will be taken care of."

Maggie stood up to leave, sensing she was being dismissed.

"One more thing. If you are not a vegetarian, during your pregnancy maintain a strict vegan diet, or...you will regret it." Maggie glanced up and expected a penetrating stare to accompany this admonishment, but Ma had already closed her eyes and slipped back into a meditative state.

When Maggie missed her next period, she did a home pregnancy test. It was positive. She expected nothing less, although she had hoped otherwise, if only briefly. It wasn't as much due to Ma's premonition as it was her own inner awareness. She was already linked with Anna and began to hear her unborn daughter speaking to her in the first weeks of her pregnancy, especially given Guru's warning regarding diet. This was a bit overwhelming at first, but Maggie would reply orally and figured her daughter got the message. When inquiring about food selections at a health food store, another shopper asked if she was talking to herself.

"I do it all the time," she reassured Maggie.

"No, I was listening to my unborn daughter who claims to be a vegan. Jesus," she blurted out before she could catch herself.

The woman was startled by this reply and hurriedly pushed her cart down the aisle. What did she expect? Maggie wondered. This was San Luis Obispo, California, not Cleveland. But she was a bit beleaguered by her situation, and for now appearances were the least of her concerns. How do you prepare for the birth of a "great soul"? she asked herself repeatedly. Maggie was already a vegetarian and celibate, or had been until her one-night stand with Thomas, and while she meditated daily and did yoga, she was definitely no saint. Well, she was who she was and Anna had chosen her for a reason, or so she reassured herself.

When Maggie went for her first prenatal checkup, Dr. Ross Martin asked if she wanted to schedule an ultrasound on the four-month visit to check on the baby's sex.

"Oh, it's girl. No need," she said.

The doctor and nurse looked at each other questioningly.

"That's your sense of it?" he asked.

"Well, it's what she tells me."

"You talk to your unborn child?" he asked with concern.

"More like she talks to me. Can you believe that?" Maggie said, shaking her head.

Again the doctor and his nurse exchanged looks, and Maggie could almost read their minds: "Hormonal."

On the way out, the receptionist asked her to fill in the father's name on a maternity form. Maggie wrote: Thomas, the Kundalini Yoga teacher. When asked for more details, she simply replied, "I heard he moved to India. No luck for me finding him there."

Shortly after her return from the ashram, Maggie started receiving a $2,000 check every month from a J. Edwards, an attorney with offices in San Francisco. She checked the ashram's website, and he was on their board of directors, and so Ma hi' Ma was indeed "watching out" for her as she had promised. This would come in handy.

When Maggie returned from summer vacation for the new school year definitely pregnant, the principal at her elementary school called her in for a consultation.

"Maggie, I wish you would've let us know you were pregnant," Mrs. Phillips said, as she sipped her morning tea. She was in her fifties, rather dowdy, with elaborate eyeglasses and a shiny-beaded neck cord.

"I was going to say something once I got settled in."

"As you can imagine, we're a little taken aback, given that you're unmarried," Phillips said.

"Is that going to be a problem?" Maggie asked, trying to keep her voice even-tempered.

"Well, not if you get married."

"No chance of that," she replied. Six months later, and Thomas had not even emailed her.

The principal nodded and continued, as if she had expected this response. "Well, I believe the teacher's union will back you, but the school superintendent does have a problem with you teaching grade-school children given your...condition."

"There's not much need for an arts and craft teacher at the high school level."

"No, I wouldn't imagine."

"Well, what do you suggest?" Maggie asked.

"We were thinking that you could take one month of paid sick leave and start your maternity leave one month early."

"Fine with me. That'll give me a month to get my classes started on projects, and the substitute can take it from there."

"I've always liked you, Maggie, and I respect that you're going to have this baby. Will you being giving it up for adoption?"

"I wish," she laughed, and felt a sharp pang in reply. "Ow, that hurt," she said, glancing down at her slightly bulging abdomen.

Mrs. Phillips smiled indulgently. Another reason she wanted to take quick action was due to the rumors circulating around town about Maggie's "state of mind," which this episode only confirmed.

"Good. I'm glad that's settled," the principal said and stood up. As she walked Maggie to the door, she added, "I hope that you can keep this between us."

"Sure. I'm glad for the extra paid time."

Mrs. Phillips smiled. "We'll get the paperwork together."

Maggie should have had J. Edwards examine the early maternity-leave papers she signed two weeks later. She wasn't feeling well that day and didn't read through the document. After she took the sick leave, her monthly paycheck was deposited into her checking account as always, but the next month she received a two-month severance package. When she read the document, Maggie found that she had unwittingly agreed to resign her position to focus on a "difficult pregnancy." She could have protested this blatant subterfuge with the teacher's union, but given that she had been able to bank Guru's monthly stipend and live on her teacher's salary for the last seven months, she decided to just drop it. She could always find another teaching job elsewhere, and preferred not to continue working for people who could be so dishonest. Maggie was not surprised to learn the following year that the superintendent and Mrs. Phillips, who had been conducting an illicit affair, were both relieved of their positions. *Instant karma*, she thought.

Chapter 2

Maggie's parents had been hardly outraged by their daughter's unwed pregnancy or by her wish to have the baby and raise it herself. Her father, Mark Langford, was a professor of medieval history at UC Santa Barbara, and her mother, Grace, was a housewife and an artist—an abstract impressionist, or so she called herself. They had two daughters. Maggie's older sister Jill was married to an architect and they lived with their son in Iowa. She was never close to her, and their temperaments couldn't be any more different. Jill had studied mathematics at Berkeley and Maggie art, and while they were in school together for one year before she graduated, they had rarely spent time together. Jill was the head of the chess club, and Maggie hung out with artistic and spiritual types, and had already started practicing yoga and studying Eastern mysticism. They drove home together that year for the Christmas holiday and proceeded to drive each other to distraction with their contrary opinions and views on just about everything.

"You think you come back in another lifetime with your 'karma' to work out?" Jill said in disbelief. "Really, Maggie. It's either heaven or hell, and nobody comes back," she insisted.

"If you look around this world, you'll find enough hell on earth to suit any Christian sinner; why go anywhere else." Jill just shook her head, her rimless glasses slipping down her red nose, and she drove on in chilled silence the rest of the way.

Maggie stayed on for the New Year's celebration while her sister had hurried back to Berkeley to spend it with her boyfriend Hank, and Maggie then caught a ride to the Bay Area with friends.

When she had told her parents about her pregnancy back in early May, Grace had wanted Maggie to come home and relax for the summer. She had always enjoyed being pampered, but she

9

decided to stay in San Luis Obispo, which was only a hundred miles north. Her childhood home with its stifling memories was no place for her to relax. And then during her third month, her outward focus began to shift and she became much more inner-directed. She started attending formal meditation classes at the yoga center, and while she had meditated for years, she now found the practice almost effortless. It helped that she was on summer vacation, unattached, and was staying mostly to herself. In class the teacher often had to nudge Maggie after everyone else had already opened their eyes. She also took a yoga class for pregnant women and found that she could do most of her customary asanas except the extreme twists. She just felt buoyant, and others remarked that she had a luminous glow around her. Of course, she had told no one about her guru's premonition, and after a few slips about talking to her unborn daughter, she kept those exchanges to herself as well. Maggie soon realized that this was the "auspicious opening" that Guru had forecasted for her, and her early doubts about having this child began to evaporate.

In July she received an invitation to visit Ma hi' Ma at the ashram, and that a car would pick her up and drive her both ways. Maggie responded that she would love to visit, but felt it was best to stay close to home and not undertake any long journeys during her pregnancy, or so she said. She was surprised weeks later when she saw a poster announcing a visit by Sri Ma hi' Ma, who would hold satsang and give blessings at the Bodhi Path Buddhist Center the first week in August. So, she thought, *If the mountain will not come to Mohammed, then Mohammed must go to the mountain.* Guru would be staying with a local devotee on his farm outside of town, and after her arrival Prema called and said a car would pick up Maggie the next afternoon for tea. Maggie was a bit apprehensive. She appreciated all that Guru had done for her — the extra money was a godsend — but she was more concerned for her unborn child. The last thing she wanted was for Guru and their community to project the same kind of high expectations on Anna that Krishnamurti had to deal with as a child, or in the future to appropriate her daughter's supposed high being to bolster even Ma's benign agenda.

When the car arrived at the farm, Prema met Maggie and ushered her through the lustrous rose garden to an elevated gazebo with a magnificent view of the surrounding countryside with its green fields and blue lake. Here Ma hi' Ma was having tea with Gary Pritchard, the landowner and longtime devotee.

"Ah, here she is," Ma said, as Maggie gingerly walked up the steps to the gazebo, holding on to the railing. She stopped at the top and bowed to her guru, with hands folded and the thumbs touching her third eye. Pritchard stood up and pulled out a chair for her, and she sat down.

"I'm so pleased to meet you, Maggie," he said taking her hand. He was in his fifties, with touches of gray hair at the temples, his blue eyes clear and his smile utterly genuine. Maggie sighed in relief.

Guru had watched this exchange and smiled. "You sigh," Ma said, her stare piercing through her devotee's cautious manner. She turned to Pritchard. "Oh, I believe Maggie thinks we have designs on her daughter."

Looking at Guru and her beaming smile, Maggie felt guilty for harboring any such reservations. She bowed her head again. "No, Ma. Just concerns that Anna be allowed to develop on her own."

"One never knows with these great souls; it takes many years for some of them to find their path, while others know immediately."

"So the pregnancy goes well?" Gary asked.

"Yes, and she's a chatty little girl," Maggie volunteered, feeling she could share this revelation with them.

Ma hi' Ma's eyebrows lifted. "So, you speak with her?"

Maggie shook her head. "She speaks to me, and even has a

preference on soya milk."

Ma clapped her hands. "Oh, how wonderful. You must tell me everything, child."

Prema brought out a teapot and filled their cups, and leaving the pot in the center of the table, she strolled away. Maggie took a sip of the yogi tea, and then placed a hand on her abdomen as the baby stirred.

"Well, apparently she likes this brand. We'll have to order some for you," Ma added.

Maggie proceeded to share several stories with them, like the one about talking to herself in the health food store, and she had a rapt audience for the next hour. After a while, Ma closed her eyes and seemed to create her own bridge to Anna, or so it appeared. When Maggie finished her last story, Ma hi' Ma opened her eyes and said that Anna had a distinguished spiritual heritage, having been both a Hindu Guru and a Tibetan Rinpoche in past lifetimes. But, while she may follow her mother's religious tradition, she eventually wants to be free to choose her own path.

Maggie started to tear up upon hearing so wisely expressed what she felt in her own heart, even as she wondered about its true source. She reached over and kissed Guru's hand. "Thank you, Ma. That is what I wish for her as well."

Ma lifted her chin and stared into the young woman's eyes. "You must trust that I want only what's best for Anna, and to prove that, I will not force any further contact and will wait for you to get in touch with us, be it months or years, but our support will continue for as long as you may need it."

There was a small gathering that evening of devotees from the area with some coming from as far south as Santa Barbara, but Maggie was treated as just one of many with no special considerations. Apparently Ma hi' Ma's premonition about Anna was also a kept secret among the three of them, not even Prema or the other attendants seemed to know. At the conclusion of the evening's festivities, everyone lined up and one by one Guru gave each of them her blessing, which included a laying on of hands and a transmission of Shakti. Maggie nearly fainted as her unborn child seemed to draw in huge amounts of the precious energy. When she opened her eyes, Ma smiled sweetly and knowingly at her. Prema volunteered to drive Maggie back to her apartment, and while the conversation was general, she sensed that Prema was curious as to Guru's unexpected visit here and Maggie's equally surprising personal summons. But nothing was made of it.

When she had started back at school in late August, Maggie found herself less bothered by the hustle and bustle that attended the startup of each school year, but when her early maternity leave turned into a permanent vacation, she was somewhat relieved to be free of teaching for now. This may have accounted for Maggie's lack of protest over her unjust dismissal, or how it had been contrived. She had come to feel that the events of her life were being orchestrated at some higher level, and she just needed to go with the flow. Her friend Leo, a musician and fellow yogi, had volunteered to be a surrogate father at Lamaze classes if she were so interested, but Maggie didn't want to gather with other pregnant women, especially those with partners, and hear their customary complaints. Since Maggie had no grievances and Dr. Martin said hers was a most uncomplicated pregnancy, she preferred to keep to herself.

When Maggie had not come home for a visit and her pregnancy was progressing and preventing travel, her parents decided to take the initiative and drove up to San Luis Obispo in mid-October. Her father was able to take a four-day weekend: his Fridays were usually free and he would have graduate students teach his Monday classes, and so they arrived midmorning, checked into their hotel, and drove by and picked up Maggie for brunch. She had had two days' notice, but given that this was the first few weeks of her sick leave, she had not had the time or inclination to thoroughly clean her apartment. Grace took immediate notice of the clutter, but said nothing given her daughter's condition.

At a local bistro with outdoor seating under a canopy of cottonwood trees, they ordered and her parents were surprised that Maggie was having a salad given the vast array of omelets and egg dishes on the menu. Her mother said something about it.

"I've gone vegan for the pregnancy," she replied.

"Aren't you concerned you won't get enough protein?" Grace asked.

"I eat lots of soya products and vegetable protein, and Dr. Martin says my blood protein levels are...adequate."

"Only adequate," her father protested. "Won't that stunt your child's brain development?"

"Not really, Dad. I trust my baby has inherited enough smart genes to handily compensate."

Mark laughed. "Flattery will get you...only a brief reprieve, my dear. Nothing more."

While they waited for their meal to be served, Grace brought up the subject that had been bothering her and that Maggie had circumvented during their recent phone conversations.

"So Maggie, you've never told us who the father is?"

Maggie hesitated, knowing this subject would be contentious, and she didn't want to quarrel with her mother about it right now. "He is a Kundalini Yoga teacher I had a brief one-night fling with. He had already left for India when I discovered I was pregnant," she added and lied, and could actually feel a physical reaction to lying. Was it Anna monitoring her, or her own increased sensitivity, she wondered.

"Well, if I'm not mistaken, there is postal service in India, and if he has a cell phone like most in your generation, you could just call him."

They were interrupted by their meal being served, and with

the attendant fill-up of coffee cups and a new hot water pot for her yogi tea, the subject was momentarily dropped, but not forgotten. After they had started eating, her father directed the conversation to how Maggie planned to spent her maternity leave and make use of the opportunity. She couldn't help but smile; her father was always the supreme utilitarian.

"Well, Dad. I won't be taking night or correspondence classes, if that's what you're getting at. I plan to paint, listen to music, do yoga and meditate to create a sacred space for my baby's development."

Her father sighed and lowered his head, concentrating on his steak and eggs, which were rather good and with plenty of animal protein.

As they finished their meal and after her husband had surrendered the conversational field, Grace once again pressed the issue. "Really, Maggie. You can barely support yourself on your teacher's salary. Raising a child by yourself without spousal support is…rather irresponsible."

Maggie didn't want to discuss her guru's stipend with them, since it would lead into an area, her premonition of Anna's sanctity, that she didn't want to share at this time. Let the child's presence be the test of that claim. Maggie just looked back at her mother with a sweet smile, and after a few moments it became clear a reply wouldn't be forthcoming.

Before Grace could press the issue further and spoil a rather pleasant outing, her father added, "Well, put his name down as the father on the birth certificate, so if you change your mind later, you'll at least have legal recourse."

Maggie turned to her father. "Yes, that would be smart."

While this wasn't an agreement to follow through on the suggestion, it was the best he could expect. "What say we head down to Pismo Beach, get a cabana, and let you get some sun?"

"Yes," Grace chimed in. "You do look rather pale."

"Sounds good to me. I don't have a bathing suit that'll fit, but

I can put on shorts and a halter top."

Her father stood, tossed a fifty-dollar bill on the table, and said, "Then it's settled."

Maggie decided to have a home birth with a midwife. She had attended the hospital births of friends' babies, and the cold sterile atmosphere of the delivery room would not be in harmony with her baby's energy, or hers for that matter. She contacted the ashram, and their outreach clinic recommended a local devotee, Megan Fairchild—*a most auspicious name for a midwife,* Maggie thought. Dr. Martin wasn't entirely pleased with her decision, but said if any pregnancy lent itself to a home birth, it was hers. Maggie also sensed that this was her child's preference as well, not that she would tell anybody about this consideration. Her parents, especially her father, were rather alarmed by this decision, given all the complications that could ensue, but Maggie promised to keep her mother posted and she would come up a week early and stay with her during the home birth.

Maggie was unable to keep this promise. One night in late November, nearly two weeks before her due date, Maggie had a dream in which a damn broke and a frolicking infant rode down the river in a life raft waving her hands. In the morning she called Megan and told her to be prepared. Shortly afterward, she felt the fetus drop into her pelvis and rotate to come out of the birth canal head first. Megan arrived as the first contractions began. The birth alert had gone out, and several local devotees hurried over and unbeknownst to Maggie, Gary Pritchard was called and he notified Ma hi' Ma.

Hours later, in what was claimed by Megan to be her most uncomplicated and easiest delivery ever, Anna Jane Langford was born in San Luis Obispo surrounded by lighted candles and Hindu chanting without a cry but with a monumental smile on her face. Mother and child were pronounced healthy, and Anna was cleaned up and wrapped in a baby blanket and placed in her mother's arms as Maggie sat up in bed. The baby girl continued to look up at her mother and to the delight of those assembled, as legend would have it, with an upward tilt of her head gazing at others of a less corporal nature, or so they assumed. Grace Langford flew up that afternoon from Santa Barbara, and her presence scattered the midwife and the few remaining devotees who lingered on, especially after she blew out all the candles "to get some oxygen in the room." Maggie was peaceful and accepting of the role her mother needed to play, but one look into her baby girl's eyes seemed to calm Grace, and she ended up holding her granddaughter and rocking both of them to sleep shortly afterward.

Chapter 3

Anna was a normal infant, or at least by outward appearances. The child had a sweet disposition and hardly ever cried to alert her mother of dirty diapers or the need to be fed. Baby books had trained Maggie to listen for these cues, but when they weren't forthcoming, and after a few embarrassing dirty-diaper comments from others, she became more vigilant and proactive. It also became obvious that Anna did not like either the noise or the energy frequency of television and would practically shiver when it was playing. Maggie permanently unplugged the TV's electric cord. While she did not view many programs, she switched to reading newspaper articles on the Internet from Google News and watched streamed programming on her laptop. Soon, however, even that need faded and the atmosphere in the house became very tranquil and almost sanctified. The ashram's female devotees in the area often came by to bring food or hand-knitted baby apparel, or just to be in the space and "soak up the vibe," as one of them articulated. Gary Pritchard called and stopped by to see the baby a week later. He asked to take a photo for Ma hi' Ma, but Anna balled up her little fists and pouted at this intrusion, and so he desisted but stayed on and rocked her to sleep, totally enchanted by Anna's "sweetness," which many had noted and which became an unofficial baby nickname.

As Anna's first Christmas approached, her parents were insistent that Maggie either drive down with her baby, or they were driving up and would take them out for dinner at a local restaurant. Maggie didn't want to spend Christmas with anybody, other than inviting a few friends over, but she had always been a dutiful daughter and felt conflicted by her reluctance to celebrate the holidays with her family. There seemed to be only one solution, and so she called Gary Pritchard and asked if he would like to drive them to the ashram for Christmas. He was delighted and readily agreed, and Ma hi' Ma took this as an overture and called to extend her welcome. Maggie asked her if she would send an invitation that she could later share with her family as the reason for her absence from their holiday festivities. Ma hi' Ma, who grew up in a large Irish family, said she understood her evasion perfectly well and they had a good laugh over their little conspiracy. Her mother was offended, but her father understood the "primacy of a religious imperative," although this was, as with most of his cultural opinions, mainly an intellectual appraisal. He also secretly wanted Jill and her family to visit, which would not happen if Maggie was present. They spoke about them coming up after the first of the year, when her father promised to look into her teacher's suspension. Maggie agreed to the visit if not to the investigation.

While this was a Hindu ashram, its guru was a Westerner and raised Christian, and so both Christmas and Easter were celebrated there as a nonsectarian show of religious tolerance and a belief in the one Spirit that all worshipped in their own way. Ma hi' Ma had agreed not to speak of her premonition about Anna, and that Maggie and her child would be treated in no special way, outside of a private audience with her. It became obvious, however, that Anna was indeed special, and devotees who had spent years "soaking up" the spiritual emanations of their guru knew the energy when they were exposed to it. At first this took the form of holding the one-month-old child and passing her around, to Ma holding Anna during the "procession," when devotees would kneel before her and receive Guru's Christmas blessing. Many claimed this offering was particularly potent that year. As with any changes or a disturbance in her routine, Anna was amazingly tolerant and her equanimity was noted as a sign of her spiritual status, which Guru finally acknowledged with Maggie's reluctant agreement. They were told that Anna had been a Hindu Guru and Tibetan Rinpoche in a past life, and

Guru left it at that.

When several of the devotees reported Anna appearing to them in their dreams, Maggie grew concerned and considered these claims as a kind of psychic contagion where overly religious people in an isolated environment project their unconscious "affects" onto each other. In this case it was her infant child—a natural focus given the Christmas season with its depictions of the manger and baby Jesus. During her pregnancy and after Anna's birth, Maggie had restrained herself and tried not to project a mother's natural expectation of high promise on her child, especially given all the signs of Anna's sanctity. She had personally dealt with her parents' hopes and wishes growing up that she follow an academic career path, despite her mother's own artistic leanings, and with their disappointment when she chose another course of study. So, Maggie decided to cut short her visit. When news of her decision came to Guru's attention, she was summoned for a private audience. She brought Anna with her, since she felt uncomfortable leaving her with any of the devotees given the heightened atmosphere the child's effusive energy had generated.

It was fairly cold even for Northern California, and Maggie and Anna were dressed in warm winter clothing, which they kept on when visiting Ma hi' Ma in her temple room. While the old mansion was heated, and there was a fire burning in the rather large and ancient stone fireplace, the atmosphere in the room was still rather chilly.

"Maggie," her guru started off, with frown lines prominent as well as pouty lips. "Anna is not strictly 'yours' in the traditional sense of mother and child, as Jesus was not Mary's. You must step back and allow the natural outpouring of her inner energy, and if that appears as dreams to others, you must accept that and even be grateful for the sign."

"And if this is just an example of the psychic contagion that happens at most ashrams, which you yourself have commented on in the past, I'm just supposed to allow this unhealthy fixation?"

Guru's frown deepened. "You should let me be the judge of that."

Maggie tried to contain herself, and she let her emotional reaction settle so as not to lash out unconsciously. "In most matters spiritual, Ma, I would be willing to abide by your judgment. And while I may be overprotective, I feel that my instincts in regard to Anna for now take precedence."

Guru actually smiled and did not take offense, or seemingly so. "Yes, every mother feels that way. I've always loved the story from Yogananda's *The Autobiography of a Yogi* when Sri Yukteswar's eighty-year-old mother asks him if he's still hanging out with those yogis." Maggie recalled that episode in Yogananda's book, one of her favorites, and was reassured.

"But, I would expect more from you, Maggie," said Guru, a smile lingering on her lips. "Let me ask you, has Anna appeared to you in your dreams?"

"No, not that I recall," Maggie reluctantly added, knowing where this line of questioning was headed. Guru did not comment on the obvious. "And so you think I'm jealous?" Again, no reply. "And has she appeared in yours?"

Guru narrowed her eyes, but did not overreact to that lack of proof. "No, but then the real question is, have I appeared in Anna's dreams?"

Maggie hesitated. Was this a trick question? "I guess we won't know until she can speak."

"Well, establish a telepathic link with Anna and ask her?"

This was galling for Maggie since she could hear Anna in her mind, but so far had been unable to establish an inner dialogue exchange with her daughter and ask questions. She figured this would come in time and that her exposure to the child's elevated energy would open such a channel.

"I'd rather just drop this inquiry," Maggie insisted.

"Just more religious hysteria?" Guru replied rather unkindly.

Maggie stood and bundled up her child. "I have always been a devoted disciple of yours and will continue to be, but I can see that there is a tug-of-war of wills going on over my child, and that I will not tolerate it. So, for now, I ask that you withdraw your financial support, and Anna and I will allow the greater universe to bring us what we need without undue obligations."

Ma hi' Ma winced, feeling somewhat contrite, but resolved nevertheless. "If you wish, but you will discover, I'm afraid, that the protection of this compound may be Anna's only refuge from a world hostile to those with a true spiritual spark." When Maggie didn't react, Guru added, "And their protectors."

"We'll see," Maggie said dismissively.

"I'm sure Gary would be glad to drive you back home tomorrow."

"If he or somebody else could just take me to the airport today, that would be more to my liking."

"As you wish, child." Guru clapped her hands and closed her eyes, indicating that this audience was over. Maggie walked out of the temple and hurried back to her lodging, calling Gary on her cell phone. He was more than glad to drive them back today, but Maggie asked if he could just take her to the Sacramento Airport, since the drive time there was shorter than to the Bay Area's large airports with the city's congested Christmas traffic.

Gary tried to dissuade her from flying back, and when he couldn't, he called his assistant and had her pull strings to book Maggie on the next available flight, and had it charged to him. Maggie protested, but he sounded so crushed that she gave in to this sweet man, innocently caught in a battle of wills between these two hardheaded women. The antiseptic air, noise, and dissonant energy of this international airport was not to Anna's liking, but once they were airborne she calmed down and seemed to enjoy the movement of the commuter jet, even the occasional jarring from air turbulence. It was a quick thirty-minute flight, and despite the unwanted attention of the woman seated next to them—an odd-looking Filipino with boundary issues—they had escaped the perceived peril of the ashram and would soon be delivered to the sanctity of their home. Anna finally fell asleep on the taxi ride from the airport, but it had been an eventful three days, one Maggie hoped not to repeat on future holiday outings.

That night, after breastfeeding Anna and putting her in the baby crib, Maggie poured herself a glass of sparkling apple cider, her alcohol substitute, and settled into her comfy chair in the living room to review the events of the last few days. She didn't like to dwell on the past, but she had made a precipitous decision that had brought more confusion instead of less into this holiday season, and she wanted to know why. Why, in fact, had she not wanted to go home was the first question? She let this inquiry settle, and the answer was not surprising: she didn't want Anna exposed to the generational dysfunction of Christmas and its typical American celebration in a family setting. Her parents were more conscious than most, but as a spiritual commentator had once said, "If you think you're enlightened, go home for Christmas." The holiday season did seem to bring up old wounds, and Anna was very sensitive to her surroundings. But then Maggie ran in the opposite direction, to the ashram where she expected a more tranquil setting and less unconscious projection. Instead she was confronted with more of both, if of a different variety. Maggie had tried to shield Anna from the outside world's intrusion but had failed miserably, and then she wondered if maybe her daughter did not need her overt protection, and this was more about her needs than Anna's. Maybe she should just let go and "let God" as it were? Was it that simple, she asked herself?

Maggie set down the wineglass, pulled the knitted comforter over her, lay back and instantly fell asleep. It was a restful sleep, and she dreamed of Anna as a precocious four-year-old, with her curly light brown locks and a button nose, but with eyes that saw everything. She reached over and took her mother's hand and brought her to the playground at the nearby park. There she jumped onto the merry-go-round and pulled her mother onto it, and it began to spin around faster and faster. Maggie was holding on for dear life, while Anna grabbed a bar with both hands and let her legs get extended out as it whirled faster and faster, and then she let go and flew through the air landing upright on her feet. Her mother was terrified that she would hurt herself, but as the merry-go-round slowed down and she jumped off, her daughter came over, took her hand and led her away, as if the parental roles were reversed. Maggie woke up and smiled. She got the message, but would she follow through with it?

Chapter 4

Maggie's teachers' union had been outraged by her dismissal, but she refused to take legal action against the school system, who claimed she breeched her contract's moral clause. While the union did find substitute teacher assignments for her with local private schools, Maggie wouldn't put Anna in daycare or hire a babysitter so she could work outside the house. One of the teachers, a devotee of Ma hi' Ma, would drop off home assignments, and so Maggie was able to bring in a little income while living off her dwindling savings from her guru's earlier stipend. She didn't apply for unemployment because of its job-search requirement. Her parents were concerned and asked that she move home with them, since they still had an unused bedroom after the girls had left for college years ago. Jill's room had been converted into a studio for Grace. Maggie said she would be just fine and that something would turn up.

She had always wanted to write a book, and given her free time Maggie penned a children's story showing how art can connect people to themselves and others. It had a subtle spiritual undertone, but she was careful to keep it secular and universal. She self-published a version on her home computer with rather elaborate illustrations and printed out color copies. The arts-and-craft teacher, who provided Maggie with freelance work, loved the book and passed it out to select students, one of whom had a father with publishing connections. The book found its way to a San Francisco publisher of children's books, Millburn Press, who offered Maggie a contract on the book, which they would republish with a few changes, and an advance with a request for a follow-up book. Maggie was delighted and thanked her spiritual guides for providing this opportunity.

For Anna's first six months, Maggie's days were otherwise spent raising her daughter. For a usually very active and creative woman, she did not find the demands of motherhood tiring or trying. In fact, this caregiving focus was as much a caring for her own feminine nature as it was for her daughter's welfare, with the added benefit that Anna's powerful spiritual energies deepened her inner life and her connection to the greater whole. Her daily tasks had become a kind of active meditation. There were carriage strolls to a nearby park, where Anna loved to watch the children playing on the swingsets and the slides. When Maggie acquired a baby sling, she could swing with her, but what Anna loved even more were strolls along the beach or sitting on a bench at the Pismo Beach Pier and looking out at the ocean on a warm day. Maggie knew that waves hitting the shore created large amounts of negative ions, or *prana* in Eastern lore, and Anna just naturally responded to this outpouring of energy. She loved the sun and being outdoors, but Maggie had to limit her exposure time. While Anna would have liked to stay out all day, or so it appeared to her, the child never pouted when it was time to go inside. She just accepted what happened and seemed pleased with the beingness of life or the "isness" of the moment as some would phrase it.

After her book's acceptance, Maggie was asked to come to San Francisco, or actually Mountain View south of the city proper, to talk with the book's editor and publisher, Jean Millburn. She was a bit apprehensive about this first foray into publishing and the exposure it would bring them. Maggie had never been what you would call a "public person," and she knew, if the book were successful, that she would have to step out into the world and speak up for herself. But, she had a child to support, and she would push herself to make the most of this opportunity. Maggie packed the car, strapped Anna into her infant car seat, and drove up the coast to the Bay Area.

Anna loved the ocean breeze coming through the window, but eventually she fell asleep and didn't wake up until they were just outside of Big Sur. Maggie pulled into a seaside park and breastfed her daughter with the sound of waves pounding against the high cliffs in the background. Afterward Maggie carried Anna over to the railing overlooking the ocean, and she appeared delighted with the ocean spray that dampened their faces and no doubt filled their lungs with negative ions. As they resumed their trek up the coast, Maggie glanced at her daughter in the rearview mirror and noticed that her eyes were closed and she was shaking or shivering. She immediately powered up all the cracked windows and turned the heat on, but Anna continued to shake with her eyelids twitching. Apparently she wasn't cold, and so Maggie became concerned that her daughter may have a nervous disorder and decided to have her checked out by her pediatrician upon their return.

They arrived at the publisher in late afternoon. It was a small second-story office above an art gallery but well appointed with a half-dozen young people engaged in various activities. Jean Millburn stepped out to the reception area and took Maggie back to her office. She was of medium height, well-proportioned, with wavy dirty-blond hair, and a wonderful smile. The hallway wall displayed a row of book covers in frames, two of which were award-winners, but Jean didn't gloat over them. Maggie was ushered into a small, sun-lit office and sat across from Jean at her desk with Anna sitting upright in her infant car seat in a chair next to her.

They talked about the book's publication; Maggie was shown page layouts, which she liked, but was concerned about the reproduction quality of the artwork.

"These are just mockups," Jean told her. "You've seen our books; they're of the highest color-printing quality."

"Yes, of course. I should've known better."

"The main challenge at this stage is the title: *Rainbow Magic*. There is a whole series of *Rainbow Magic* books, and so we need to come up with something original."

"Darn. Rainbow arcs are how Lisa sees the children connecting through their artwork."

"Yes, but it's about 'connecting,' however it is interpreted."

They sat and thought about an alternative title while Anna kept looking back and forth between them, as if she could see the rainbows of energy connecting all three of them. Suddenly, Maggie had a thought. "How about *Life Lines*."

Jean smiled. "Yes, that's great. Let me see." She searched Amazon under children's books. "No, nothing with that title." She thought a moment. "How about *Lisa's Lifelines*?"

Lisa was the main character who could see the invisible connections between herself and others, which appeared as thin colored strings, or rainbows. "Can we still use the rainbow strings?"

"Yes, but see if you can't weave this 'lifeline' theme into the text."

Maggie nodded her head. "Yes, I can do that."

Jean called Barry Howell, her art director, into the office. He was in his late twenties with straight blond hair and the loose limbs of a surfer. She introduced him to Maggie and told him the suggested new title. He liked it and said he could come up with some mocked-up covers tomorrow. They then settled into an editorial meeting as Jean told her about changes she would like in regards to both story and character development. Maggie agreed with most of them and made a good case for those she didn't particularly like. She also didn't want to homogenize the spiritual import of the theme, and her publisher finally agreed to that. It was five o'clock, and Jean said she was taking them to dinner, and as they had arranged earlier, Maggie and Anna would spent the night with her. "I hope you like Chinese, because Cupertino, where I actually live, has some really good restaurants with its Asian population." Maggie nodded her head as she gathered up Anna. "Or, you could leave your car here, and we could drive into San Francisco?"

Maggie stood up with Anna in her arms. "It was a long trip,

and we're pretty tired. A Chinese restaurant near your home sounds just great."

"Okay. Would you like Barry to join us?"

Maggie smiled. Why did everybody want to fix her up with colleagues or friends? "I'd rather something quieter with just the three of us."

Jean did a double-take. "Oh, you mean Anna as the third."

"Yes, you'll find she has a rather strong presence."

Dinner was delightful, and Maggie learned that Jean had graduated from UC Berkeley where she got her master's in English and then went through Boston College's publishing program before securing an assistant editor's job in New York. She was fortunate enough to have started in 2002, a few years before the 2008-2009 economic crash that decimated publishing and its personnel. At that point Jean moved back to the Bay Area and worked for several small publishers, before opening her own shop.

While she was telling her story, Jean occasionally glanced at Anna in her car seat; she was staring at them as if she were following the conversation. This became unnerving after a while. "Maggie, your baby seems unusually captivated by a conversation she can't possibly be following."

Maggie laughed. "Of course not, but she seems pretty attuned to people's energy and its expression, as if she can see their auras or something."

Jean was amused by this statement. "Maybe this is where you got the rainbow idea for your book...watching her with others."

Maggie stuck her finger out and Anna grabbed hold of it. "So, Anna, if that's so, you can start to think about mommy's next book."

She smiled and gurgled and acted in a typical baby manner. Maggie had noticed this "baby routine" on occasion, especially when she had detected an unusual level of interest in Anna's reaction to the goings-on around her. She tried not to project too much onto the situation, but it was intriguing. Maggie just assumed that Anna had a strong spirit-body connection, which could sometimes come through more clearly than it did with older children and adults locked into their mindsets, and that directed her actions.

After dinner Maggie followed Jean to her house, a lovely two-story adobe-style home on a tree-lined street, and they chatted for a while before retiring early. Jean said they'd leave in the morning around 8:00 a.m., so it was best to meet up for breakfast around 7:15 or so.

Maggie and Anna, dressed for their drive home, made their breakfast appointment but Jean was late. After a while Maggie went out to the front porch with Anna and they sat on the divan; Maggie breastfed her baby while sipping a cup of tea and just being in the moment. Fifteen minutes later Jean trudged down the stairs, fixed a cup of instant coffee from the still-warm kettle, and joined them on the porch.

"My apologies. I slept right through the alarm. Don't ever remember doing that."

"Apparently you needed the sleep."

Jean nodded her head. "I had the most peculiar dream. There was a book launch party at a high-end restaurant, and my assistant, who I expected to bring out copies of our new book, wheeled out a bassinette with a newborn baby instead."

Maggie had to laugh. "Have you been thinking of having a baby?"

"No. I'm definitely a career woman." She set down her cup and put out her arms, and Maggie handed Anna to her. She sat down on the divan with this bundle of joy. "But, if they are all as calm and self-possessed as little Anna here, I might reconsider."

Maggie was tempted to share with Jean her guru's belief about Anna's spiritual lineage, but she had promised herself to keep this a secret between the two of them, or at least among the small community of Ma hi' Ma's select devotees. She figured that the time would come for full disclosure as Anna grew older, and Maggie wrote more books for this publisher.

Jean gazed into Anna's eyes and was transfixed for a moment. She looked over at Maggie. "I just had an image of myself in another era, possibly in Italy, with a bevy of young children." She handed Anna back to her mother. "What's with this daughter of yours, and her affect on me?" This seemed like a rhetorical question, and so Maggie didn't answer.

Jean stood up. "We're late, or I'm late." She paused for a moment. "I think we're finished at the office, so I'll just drive by the south entrance to Route 85 and you can take it from there." She stepped over and gave Maggie and Anna a sideways hug.

Maggie thought they still had things to sort out, but didn't say anything. Jean had had a powerful reaction to Anna and her spiritual energies, and it was best that she let the woman sort this out without further stimulation. "Actually, I'm going to drive north on 280 and take the mountain road to Half Moon Bay and head back from there on Route 1. Anna so liked the coast drive up to Monterey; I thought I'd treat her."

Jean smiled. "My favorite spot in the whole area." She went inside to retrieve her briefcase, locked up the house, and walked them to their car. "I so enjoyed this, Maggie...and Anna," she added, holding out her little finger that Anna grabbed. "So, when you've made the editorial changes, I'll have the final manuscript copyedited and email a file for you to go over."

"And the covers Barry was mocking up?"

"Oh, that's right. Well, maybe..."

"Jean, just email me jpegs and I'll give you my feedback." Jean appeared discombobulated by this oversight, but got in her car without further word and waited for Maggie to back out of the driveway, and on the street she pulled around her and they drove off together.

The drive over the mountains and then down the coast from Half Moon Bay was spectacular, and Anna stayed awake all the way to Monterey. While Maggie stared at the ocean out the window, she thought about how much her daughter's energies affected people and that she needed to be more cognizant of this influence. She must have a very strong aura, Maggie thought, and as she grew older would need to pull it in closer to her body when they were out in public. She would take this up with her once they established a communication.

Chapter 5

Maggie had kept her teacher's health insurance and paid the premiums after her dismissal, and so she could follow up with her pediatrician about Anna's supposed nervous disorder. At Anna's six-month checkup with Dr. Martin, she expressed her concerns.

"What signs did you note?"

"Well, sometimes she closes her eyes and just shakes, and you can see her eyes moving behind her eyelids as if she were in REM."

"Infants do spend eighty percent of their sleep in REM."

"But she's fully awake when this occurs," Maggie added.

"How long do these episodes last?"

"They vary, often just a few minutes, but they seem to be getting longer and I'm concerned."

"Well, cerebral palsy, or CP, is usually caused by prenatal brain damage, and since this was a home birth, let's be cautious." He paused a moment and looked at Anna. "Have you noticed any muscle control or coordination problems?" he asked.

"No, nothing like that. She seems perfectly normal and healthy, outside of these episodes."

"Well, let me test her reflexes and coordination, and check her posture, which are early symptoms."

Dr. Martin ran a few simple tests that Maggie observed, which all resulted in normal healthy responses. "There's nothing that I can detect. If these 'episodes' continue, I can refer you to a neurologist and they can do an MRI, but I wouldn't suggest doing that yet. Let's just keep a close eye on her development. A CP diagnosis is rarely done before two years of age."

"Okay. Believe me, last thing I want is to expose her to any invasive technology, but her welfare is my prime consideration."

It occurred to Maggie in the weeks ahead, as she observed her baby's gentle swaying motion during these episodes, that there might be a spiritual explanation for them—Ma hi' Ma's trance states were an example of that. She didn't want to ask Guru, so she read biographies of several Hindu and Buddhist saints and was particularly heartened by reading about the ecstatic trance states of Ramakrishna and more recently Anandamayi Ma who passed in 1982. She ordered a book about the life of this famed Hindu saint replete with photos of her as a young girl in *samadhi*, and wondered if her daughter as an infant was experiencing euphoric states similar to hers. This was an exciting as well as a daunting prospect. She doubted that kindergarten class would allow ecstatic-trance breaks for the highly evolved. It occurred to Maggie that she might have to homeschool Anna, and while that consideration was years away, she would check out the state requirements and see if she needed to get a broader teaching certificate to qualify.

Maggie and Jean had decided on a cover for *Lisa's Lifelines*, and advance galleys were sent out that summer. Jean was overjoyed by the response and was assured of stellar reviews, but what was equally encouraging were the advance orders from Barnes and Noble, the last big national bookstore chain, and from a slew of independent bookstores specializing in children's books. Jean had talked to Maggie about her publicity obligations, but she didn't realize that in the fall it would require her to do a book tour starting in Northern California and then flying to several major cities around the country. This presented a problem. Could she take her then ten-month-old infant with her? Jean assured her that the tour would be much too tasking to bring Anna. Maggie realized that the only alternative was to allow her parents to take care of her for the two-week sprint in late October. While her parents had visited her twice since her daughter's birth, Maggie decided to spend a weekend with them in early August to test the waters, as it were, before asking them to watch her while she toured.

The occasion or excuse was the galley release of her book. Maggie figured if the visit turned into a disaster, she would have plenty of time to figure out an alternative plan, like hiring a nanny to travel with them and stay with Anna in hotel rooms for media events, or sit with her at bookstore signings. Grace was thrilled by the proposed visit and her father, who had published a half-dozen books in his field, was eager to welcome another author into the family. He did insist she return on the book's publication for a signing at Chaucer's Bookstore, where he himself had had several signings and which had a large children's department. She copied the email to Jean, who said her publicity gal would set it up. Maggie had a galley sent directly to her parents from the publisher. Her mother immediately responded; she loved the artwork and the story was "very imaginative." Her father, an academic, was less enthusiastic, or so she assumed since he didn't respond.

Maggie had been gradually introducing solid food into Anna's diet at six months while continuing to breastfeed her; she would do both until Anna was ready to handle a strictly solid-food diet. She bought both vegan and regular baby food, and discovered that Anna definitely preferred the vegan brand. Maggie found a vegan soya milk formula that she seemed to like, and her mother could bottle-feed her while she was away, interspersed with meals of baby food. She was concerned that her father as a meat eater might try to interfere and insist that her daughter be introduced to meat or diary, which was the only source of complete protein. Again, one of the reasons for this visit was to test their resistance to the established order of Anna's life and Maggie's preferences. If her daughter wanted to eat meat, it would be fine with her, but at this point she wouldn't even take formula made with cow's milk, so she figured that Ma hi' Ma's injunction was prescient in this regard.

The appointed time for the visit arrived, and Maggie placed Anna in her infant car seat and put her stroller and a supply of vegan formula and baby food in the trunk. She drove down Highway 101, which was an inland road until it merged with Route 1 on the coast just north of Santa Barbara, much to Anna's delight. Her parents actually lived in Goleta where the university was located but only a few miles from the city proper. It was Saturday, which she chose since her father would be home for the weekend. She drove up to their ranch-style house with its blue-shingled exterior in the foothills of the Santa Ynez Mountains, and her parents came out to greet them. Grace unhooked Anna from the car seat and lifted her up into her arms.

"I fixed your old room up with a crib."

Maggie looked at her in amazement as she was unloading their bags from the trunk. "You don't still have ours?"

"Dear me, no. A young couple on the block lent us theirs. Her son has outgrown it."

"Here, let me help you," her father said, as she handed him the luggage bags. Maggie removed a small box of baby food jars. "What's that?"

"It's Anna's vegan baby food." He rolled his eyes. "Okay, Dad. Let's not make this an issue." He shook his head, swung the bags over his shoulder and hand-carried the box into the house.

"He promised me, but you know your father," Grace said, then added, "A box? You're just staying for the weekend, right?"

"Thought I might store some here for future visits."

Grace nodded her head, and they walked through the house to the patio, its table and chairs under an umbrella cover, with a spectacular view of the mountains. Maggie breastfed Anna while her mother updated her on their life and what was happening with her sister Jill, who was having a rough patch with her husband.

"Well, I don't know how partners can get along with each other without a spiritual foundation to their relationship; in time it all comes down to ego battles," Maggie added.

Her mother sighed deeply. "It does take perseverance." She smiled. "Speaking of which, have you informed Anna's father about her birth?"

"I got a postcard from him asking how I was doing. Since I never gave him my address, I'm sure word got back to him along with my contact info through the yogi grapevine, and while he asked about the baby, I didn't reply." Actually Maggie had wondered if Ma hi' Ma hadn't initiated this contact hoping to use Thomas to make a claim on Anna, since she had not been in touch with her guru since last Christmas. If this was the only reason for his outreach, she was rather perturbed by his late weakhearted inquiry. Fortunately, she had not taken her father's advice to name him on the birth certificate as the father. Of course he could at some point insist on a DNA paternity test, but she sensed that Thomas would not force the issue or be so easily manipulated.

"Don't you think he has a right to know that he's the father?" Grace asked.

"A one-night stand with no follow-up until a year and a half later doesn't in my mind give him any rights."

Suddenly Anna gummed her breast rather hard. Maggie glanced down at her daughter and wondered if this was a response to her exclusion of Thomas in their life, a reaction that was a bit unnerving.

"He may feel differently."

"Well, he has our address and can come calling if he likes, and I'll take it from there."

Grace nodded her head. This was about as cooperative as she could hope on this issue from her willful daughter. "Well, Anna must be tired, or maybe both of you. You may want to take a nap before the afternoon barbecue?" Maggie gave her mother a questioning look. "Your father wants to show off his granddaughter to his friends and neighbors."

Maggie was about to object but realized that she couldn't

control everything in regard to her daughter's exposure to the outside world and would just have to allow the "isness" of life to bring what it will to their doorstep. "Yeah, I think I'll put Anna down, and lie down myself."

The lawn party was much as she had expected, about twenty people and a half-dozen children who ran about but mostly played in the pool. Maggie had dressed Anna in her best white outfit with a small sunbonnet, and she seemed to be delighted with all the attention and activity. Since there were no inquires about a husband or the child's father, Maggie assumed that her mother had passed the word that the subject was verboten. The only real dispute was her not allowing others to hold her daughter, as much for their sake as Anna's, and so she put the baby in the stroller and let her parents' friends squat down to engage her or wheel her around the yard.

Sitting down at a table drinking a glass of iced tea and picking at the grilled vegetables her father had prepared for her, Maggie talked with a neighbor who had an eleven-month-old baby boy.

"Anna has the most pleasant disposition. Does she ever cry or carry on?" Elizabeth asked.

"No. She seems content about whatever happens around her. I even have to watch her feeding schedule, because she never cries when hungry."

"Boy, are you lucky. My Andrew is a real terror and won't give either of us a moment's rest." She noticed that they had not brought the baby to the outing. The woman answered Maggie's questioning look. "His grandmother has him for the afternoon. I didn't want to inflict him on others." She thought, with that kind of attitude, no wonder he's an angry child.

Later on, while holding Anna and just watching everybody, Maggie could tell that this was about as quiet and laidback a gathering of her parents' friends as she could imagine. She remembered such parties growing up in which this was not always the case. Finally her mother came over and sat down next to them.

"Everybody seems to be on their best behavior today, and we're going to have plenty of beer left over. It's must be Anna; she seems so genteel that they don't want to disturb her equanimity."

Maggie smiled, but said nothing.

Chapter 6

On Sunday morning Maggie had placed Anna on a blanket in the middle of the living room floor while she read the newspaper. Grace walked in with a cup of coffee and sat down in a chair and watched her granddaughter sitting there ignoring the baby toys they had bought for her visit, just being happy and content. After a while Anna began to sway her head and seemed to shiver. Immediately Grace stood up to retrieve a small baby blanket and wrapped it around her shoulders. Anna soon fluffed it off as her grandmother sat there and stared at the child.

"Maggie, if she's not cold, what is she doing?"

She put down the paper and watched Anna for a long moment. "Yeah, I noticed that myself and thought she may have cerebral palsy, but Dr. Martin checked her out and said she was perfectly normal."

"Then, what is it?" she asked with concern.

Mark came into the room and plopped down next to Maggie on the sofa and picked up the front section of the Sunday paper. Noticing his wife and daughter watching the baby, he turned his attention to her.

"What's going on with her? Is she cold or something?" Mark asked.

Maggie had been reluctant to share her speculation about Anna's ecstatic states with her parents, but didn't know any other option or any cogent white lie that would suffice. "My erstwhile guru Ma hi' Ma claims Anna is an advanced soul, and I figure it's some kind of ecstatic state."

Her father laughed. "You mean like Indian yogis?"

She turned to him and replied in a straightforward, serious tone. "Yes. I did some research and this is not unusual for spiritually precocious children."

Mark shook his head. "You've been hanging out with the

New Agers for too long. You need to get the baby checked out."

"As I told mom, I had her pediatrician examine Anna and he found her perfectly healthy."

"Well, if you think that's healthy behavior, both of you need to have your heads examined," he said in a huff, then stood up and charged out of the room.

Grace was pained by her husband's reaction. "Please, forgive your father. He always looks for rational explanations."

"I know, Mom. I grew up in this household." Maggie smiled at her mother and went back to reading the newspaper, but she decided to take Anna with her on the book tour, and just hoped the money would be available for her to hire a nanny to travel with them.

Her publisher was not at all pleased with Maggie's decision, but she was adamant and would not leave Anna with anybody else. Since the schedule was already fixed, there was nothing Jean could do but go along with her stubborn author.

"You know I can't afford to send anybody along with you, or pay for other accommodations," she had told Maggie on the phone.

"I understand. I'm hiring a nanny to come with us, and she'll just stay in the same room."

"Well, at least I can get Betty to change the room reservations to double occupancies, and since infants fly for free, I'll just have her book a second adult, but you'll have to reimburse us."

"That's fine."

There was a long pause on the other end of the line. The advance sales on the book were quite good, and Jean wanted to be reasonable. "Look, I'll take the added expense out of your first royalty check."

"Jean, that's very kind of you," she said, especially since the book would have to earn back its advance before a royalty was due.

Maggie spread the word in the community that she was

inquiring about a nanny to accompany her and Anna on a book tour. Her midwife, Megan Fairchild, called and said she'd love to go along with them. They worked out a fair compensation rate for her time. Megan had gotten the schedule first and asked if she could visit her parents in Chicago on the stop there, and agreed that this stopover would be part of the payment. As the date approached, Maggie received the ashram's fall newsletter and found that her children's book was featured along with her tour schedule, with Ma hi' Ma personally requesting devotees across the country to show up at the signings and buy a book.

And then the first box of books arrived at her apartment, and Maggie tore into it to retrieve her copy. The color printing was exquisite from the covers to the illustrations, and she couldn't be more pleased with it. Like most first-time authors, she felt a certain amount of validation, and not only for herself but for her spiritually precocious child. She was making a subtle statement about Anna's connection to the greater whole of life, and would see how the book's surrogate main character was received. Maggie immediately sat Anna on her lap and read the book to her. Maybe it was just her imagination, but the baby seemed delighted with the story as it unfolded and appeared to wave her hands at the appropriate times. This was a bit more cognizance than Maggie had anticipated, and had to wonder about the true nature of her child's development and what lay in store for them in the future.

The first stop on the book tour was at the City Lights Bookstore in San Francisco, one of Maggie's all-time favorites from her college years at Berkeley. She didn't realize that they even had a young adult and children's section, because it was perceived by most as a hip bookstore for poetry and avant-garde literature. The turnout was quite good, bolstered by Ma hi' Ma's devotees in the area and from the ashram, which was only sixty miles northeast of the city. Santa Rosa, the nearest "big" city, had a

Barnes and Noble, but the population base was still considered too small by the publisher to book it for the tour.

Maggie sat at a table autographing books, with Megan in a chair next to her holding Anna. The devotees did create somewhat of a stir when, after receiving their signed books, they would next step over in front of Anna and bow their heads in homage. It was too late for Maggie to dissuade this public demonstration, and at one point a housewife dragging along her six-year-old daughter asked, "What's with the baby-Buddha thing."

Maggie looked her straight in the eye. "Beats me."

As the line thinned out and the book signing was coming to an end, there was one more customer. Ma hi' Ma stepped up to the table and set her book down. Maggie glanced up to ask the next person their name and was taken aback to discover her guru standing there.

"Does the cat got your tongue, Maggie," she said with a sly smile.

"Ma. How nice of you to come."

"Well, I heard that Anna might be in attendance as well, and I couldn't miss the opportunity to say hello to both of you."

"Of course." Maggie signed Ma hi' Ma's book, and then stood up and took Anna from Megan and handed her to Ma. Megan vacated her chair and let Guru sit down and hold the baby. Some of the devotees still in the store gathered around, and Maggie gave them a stern look to behave themselves, but the energy created by the two spiritual luminaries was almost palpable.

Ma turned to Maggie. "Dear, she is so precious. Megan tells me she goes into ecstatic trances already?"

As the bookstore manager came over to close down the signing, Maggie turned to Ma. "Maybe we should move this get-together to a restaurant."

Ma stood up holding Anna and seemed unwilling to let her go. "Yes. Excellent idea."

Megan suggested that they head over to the nearby vegan

restaurant, Millennium. Prema pulled the car around and drove them over to the restaurant while Ma continued to hold Anna, with Maggie sitting next to them in the back seat.

Ma turned to Maggie. She nodded her head. "Yes, to answer your question. At first I thought she might have cerebral palsy until I read a book on the life on Sri Anandamayi Ma."

"Yes, but even she didn't fall into trance states until she was a little older."

"Well, it's already created a rift with my parents who were going to keep Anna while I was on tour."

Ma smiled. "My husband, before we broke up, thought they were hysterical fits and wanted to hospitalize me."

Maggie glanced over at Ma hi' Ma and realized somewhat reluctantly that Guru might not only offer solace but worthwhile advice on raising her spiritually advanced child. They arrived at the restaurant where another devotee had gone ahead of them and secured a large banquet table and private room. They waited in the car until they were ready to receive them.

Ma turned to Maggie, who was getting antsy waiting to go inside. "Get used to it, dear. Like it or not, Anna is special and will require special considerations."

Maggie was not yet ready to accept that decree, but she trusted that the way would be made clear for Anna and her needs and that she merely needed to look for and follow the signs. At the restaurant Maggie breastfed Anna, and when finished she ate a large tossed salad. They sat next to Ma at the head of the table, and she listened to the conversation about the ashram and its events and news. It was a pleasant gathering and a much more suitable entertainment venue than a backyard barbecue with academics, and it made Maggie reconsider her estrangement from Ma and the ashram. She would wait until after the tour to make any firm decisions in that regard. What was encouraging was that Ma did not press her on that point, and they parted after dinner with a big hug and mutual bows.

After several more signings in the Bay Area, they flew to Seattle and one of the last buyers in the signing line was Thomas. Anna practically jumped off Megan's lap when her father knelt down in front of her clutching his book.

He turned to Maggie. "Can I hold her?" She nodded her head. Thomas set his book down on the table and picked Anna up and held her in his arms. He looked at her with absolute delight. "You can see her glow. So, what the ashram groupies are telling me is true?" he asked.

"Yeah, well last Christmas I had to cut short my visit because of their projections," she replied. Thomas continued to gaze at Anna, and didn't reply to Maggie's unkind slight.

"Yes, Ma hi' Ma's early claim of her preternatural state seems true, but I'm not making it public."

Thomas nodded his head. "That wouldn't be wise. Look what happened to Krishnamurti." He kissed Anna on her forehead and handed her back to Megan. "Maggie, while I'm obviously the father, I'll make no claims. When the two of you are interested in more contact, and if I'm ready, we'll see what happens."

"My feelings exactly," Maggie replied, yet expecting a bit more in the way of support.

"Right now, I'm off to India again for an advanced course in the *Subagh Kriya*, or yoga for prosperity and good fortune."

Maggie smiled, but didn't say what she was thinking: It's a good start toward becoming more responsible.

Thomas left without a dinner invitation, or any attempt to connect further with them while they were in town, and Maggie felt that was best for now, but she couldn't help but watch Anna's eyes follow her father out of the store. If just for Anna's sake, she would need to reach out to him, but time would tell.

Chapter 7

On their Chicago tour stop, the book signing at Barnes and Noble on State Street coincided with the only opportunity Megan would have to visit with her family, and so Maggie took charge of Anna and sat her in a borrowed car seat next to her as she signed books. There were fewer of Ma hi' Ma's devotees in line, all of whom made their customary fuss over Anna; this was much more of a big-city crowd. However, as the signing went on, Maggie noticed a tall gentleman with a blue turban and a brown beard standing off to the side watching them. He appeared to be a Sikh, and his wife and their two children with their white turbans stood in line and Maggie signed their book. Afterward while the store manager was breaking down the signing table and packing up the extra unsold books, the man stepped over while his wife and children stayed back. He was dark-skinned and introduced himself as Ashar Singh.

"Miss Langford, I had a chance to look over your book, and I found it most interesting."

"I hope your children enjoy it."

"I'm sure they will. I've also noticed a lot of Hindus in your line."

"Yes, they are devotees of my guru Ma hi' Ma."

"So you are a practicing Hindu?" Maggie wasn't sure about this man's line of questioning. He detected her discomfort. "I ask, because in India Sikhs have traditionally had a good relationship with Hindus."

"Yes, especially after Guru Bahadur was killed by the Mughals for protecting Hindus who refused to convert to Islam."

"Ah, so you've studied Indian history?"

"I've studied the history of religion and have always been impressed by the Sikh doctrine of equality for women."

"Yes, a source of conflict with our Islamic brothers," he said rather wearily. "I see that you are unaccompanied, and my wife and I would like to take you to dinner. There is an Indian restaurant, Gaylord, just a few blocks away."

Maggie paused to feel out this invitation. Ashar waved his wife and children over. She looked down at Anna who was intently watching the man. She took this as a sign of interest.

"That would be most gracious of you. But, we have to make it an early night. We leave for New York in the morning."

"Yes, of course. We will drop you at your hotel afterward." He paused for a moment. "Oh, this is my wife Nipa..."

"Kaur," Maggie added, familiar with the Sikh custom of women having the same surname of Kaur, which means princess.

Ashar smiled. "And my two boys, Badi and Fahmi, who unlike their names are very American." The boys stuck out their hands and Maggie shook them. She placed Anna in her stroller, and they walked out of the store and headed for Gaylord.

As they stepped into the restaurant, Maggie was taken aback by its classy décor and its white tablecloths, and realized that this was one of the finer ethnic restaurants in Chicago. As they were being led to their table, Maggie asked if they could be seated along the wall.

"I breastfeed my baby, and it's less...disruptive if I'm off to the side."

The hostess smiled. "Yes, of course," she said, and took them to one of the tables against the wall, seating Maggie with her back to the open room.

As they were seated, she asked Nipa, "I hope you don't find that inappropriate."

"No, not at all. And if my boys stare, they can wait in the bathroom."

Ashar gave his boys a stern look; they seemed to get the message. "We are lacto vegetarians, but they serve a wide variety of meat and fish dishes. Whatever you like."

"I'm a vegetarian, and I just love Indian food."

They ordered, and the waitress brought out some naan, and they all helped themselves, the boys buttering their bread.

Maggie breastfed Anna with the flap of the baby's blanket covering her breast. While they waited for their dinner, Ashar took this opportunity to ask about her background and interest in Hinduism and how that evolved. She told how the early practice of yoga and meditation naturally drew her to Buddhism and Hinduism, and while she could have studied either, she had met Ma hi' Ma while attending college—her ashram was only sixty miles north of the city—and weekend retreats there led to her becoming a devotee. She ended her story as she finished feeding Anna. Maggie situated her daughter on her lap, and looked around ready to answer any other questions.

"So, you are familiar with energy cords and auras and the like," Ashar asked her tentatively.

"Yes, and you wondered if rainbow lines in my story had a deeper meaning?"

Ashar and Nipa smiled. But, before he could continue, dinner was served. He asked Maggie if they could place all the dishes in the center of the table buffet style and let everybody just help themselves? Maggie agreed, and they passed around the basmati rice bowl and picked from one vegetable dish after another.

It was a delightful dinner, and while they ate Ashar and Nipa told her their backgrounds: Ashar's family had emigrated here from Amritsar, Punjab, India when he was a teenager—his father was a furniture importer. He later took over his business and expanded it and now takes frequent trips to India and Southeast Asia. Nipa was born and raised here in America by Sikh parents and studied sociology in college.

"Yes, I've always wanted to go to India, and when Anna's older, I will take her with me."

"Well, you should stay in touch with Nipa. I have many contacts there, families that would be glad to host you."

"That's particularly kind of you," Maggie said, a bit taken

aback. She couldn't help but notice the "coincidence" of Thomas returning to India and them meeting up with this Indian family with contacts in the country. This had her again thinking about India as a possible future home for them, or at least for an earlier visit than she had planned.

Ashar smiled. "I spoke with one of the Hindu women in the book line, and she told me a little about your Anna and the prophecies about her. And I would be doing my friends a favor. While we believe in equality of all under god, we do believe in great souls, and just looking at Anna I can see what the woman speaks of."

Maggie set down her fork, paused to control her reaction, and then stared the man in the eyes. "Ashar, I appreciate your kindness, but I try to keep a…lid on that kind of speculation, for Anna's sake."

Nipa leaned over and touched her arm. "Yes, I understand. And my husband only seeks to be of service to the greater unfolding of all."

Maggie looked in the woman's eyes and felt bad that she had questioned her husband's…enthusiasm. "Sorry, but it's important for me that Anna not be…specialized, I think the word is."

Ashar bowed his head. "Of course. So, no more talk of that. Maybe you can share with my boys your understanding of Hinduism, since like with all religions we Sikhs can be overly focused on our own precepts." As the dinner plates were taken up and Ashar ordered coconut ice cream for the boys and rice pudding for them. Instead of giving them a survey course on Hinduism, Maggie talked about what appealed to her, like reincarnation and the concept of karma that it shared with Sikhism, and avoided aspects of the religion like fasting, rituals, and a tendency toward idol worship that the Sikhs denounce. Their parents appreciated her sensitivity to these differences. Afterward as they waited at the front for Ashar to retrieve their car, Nipa asked if she could hold the baby. Maggie handed her over, and the woman closed her eyes and seemed to absorb Anna's energy.

On handing Anna back to her mother, Nipa, said. "While holding her, I kept seeing images of Anandamayi Ma, the Hindu saint."

"You know of her?" Maggie asked, a little overwhelmed by the continued references to this saint that kept popping up.

"Yes, I've always admired her simplicity and saintliness and have read books about her."

"I have the Lipski pictorial biography," Maggie added, and left it at that without any reference to Anna's trance states.

After Ashar and Nipa dropped her off at the Sheraton and exchanged contact information, Maggie took Anna back to their room. Megan was still out with her parents, and Maggie lay down on the bed with the baby lying on her chest as she allowed the energy of the evening and her contact with this Sikh family to wash over her. As much as she sought to isolate Anna from this kind of goodwill attention, it seemed to seek her out. Maybe living in an ashram where she could contain it might be best for her daughter, but then she immediately dismissed this prospect. She sensed that Anna wanted to live in and be part of the greater world, which would allow for her own natural development and bring these kinds of rich encounters into her life. For all she knew Ashar might put her in contact with somebody who could be very important to Anna's development at some point. While she believed in synchronicity, or the seemingly chance encounters that connected people and events at a deeper or a higher level, Anna's energies seemed to precipitate them as an almost daily event. Maggie could only shake her head; their journey together was going to be "some ride."

Chapter 8

Anna's first birthday was a quiet affair. Megan and a few of the local Ma devotees stopped over and brought gifts, and then Gary Pritchard surprised everybody by coming by and offering to take the group to dinner. Maggie noticed how Anna's eyes lit up at the sight of the older man, and she accepted the invitation on everyone's behalf. They drove to the Shalimar Indian Restaurant on Broad Street. Anna was now eating solid food more often, and Maggie smashed some of her eggplant and green peas for her daughter's meal. Gary did mention that he was driving up to the ashram for their Christmas celebration, and wondered if Maggie and Anna would accompany him. Maggie didn't make a snap decision, but told him that she would consider it. She asked about Ma and the ashram, and was told that as far as he could tell everything was as it had been for years, but that Ma was attracting more influential devotees including a film star or two.

Maggie smiled. She hoped this wasn't intended as an inducement. The last thing she wanted was to expose Anna to the celebrity circuit, not that any of them were less devout or sincere in their religious aspirations. But, they did create a certain "specialized" aura that she was trying to avoid in regards to her spiritually precocious child. Afterward Gary dropped everybody back at her house, and the others departed leaving Maggie to put Anna down for the night and consider this opening that was being presented to them. Maggie knew that Ma hi' Ma wanted to be part of Anna's life, and that having prophesized her arrival, she could stake a claim to her connection with the child. Maggie was now prepared to honor that, but did not want to expose Anna to the heightened atmosphere of another Christmas celebration there. A few days later, she called Gary and declined his kind invitation, but said after the first of the year she would drive up and spend some time at the ashram with Ma.

But the holiday season's big news was the success of Maggie's book *Lisa's Lifelines*, which made the *New York Times* Children's Picture Books bestseller's list, appearing at number eight. Jean Millburn called the Monday after its notation, and Maggie immediately went out and bought a copy of the Sunday edition. Jean also asked if she had thought of a follow-up book. Maggie said she was calling it *Heart Lines* which her publisher loved. She also phoned her mother and father, both of whom were delighted. But, of course, this brought up a renewed invitation to spend Christmas with them. After her last visit in August, Maggie had begged off on a book signing at Chaucer's Bookstore saying that she was too exhausted from the cross-country book tour. Her mother added, as an inducement of sorts, that Jill and her family weren't coming this year. This only made Maggie feel guilty about her estranged relationship with her sister, a fence she planned to mend. She accepted their invitation, much to her parents' delight, and said she'd drive down with Anna on Christmas Eve.

As the day approached, she received another surprise: a postcard from Thomas in India, saying how much he liked the ashram and the advanced Kundalini Yoga practices he was learning. Maggie noted that he didn't press her for a further connection, and just left it at that. But thoughts of Thomas and their night together did arouse her, and she realized that in focusing on Anna's development, she might have neglected her own. She made a resolution to start back with her yoga discipline after the first of the year, and would probably enroll in a Kundalini Yoga class at the Center to help raise the energy from her lower chakras. At this thought Anna threw her rubber toy across the room for emphasis, or so Maggie entertained. Talk about projections, she said to herself.

Driving up to her parents' house on Christmas Eve was a sheer delight; from the back seat Anna could see all the houses lit up with their multicolored lights as they threaded their way through the neighborhood. The displays were spectacular, and Anna was mesmerized by the lightshow. At the house Grace and Mark help her unload their luggage and gifts, and when they stepped inside, Maggie was taken aback by the large fully decorated Christmas tree. Her parents had stopped that tradition after the girls had gone off to college, but while she had missed last year's festivities, she assumed they had decorated a tree for Jill's little boy and had just kept the ornaments.

"The tree looks wonderful, Mother," Maggie said, holding Anna and taking her for a tour around it and letting her touch the ornaments. On closer inspection she spotted the lighted angel at the top and smiled: this looked new and was possibly a peace offering over their row about Anna's trance states.

At dinner Maggie made her own concession to a more peaceful holiday visit. "On the book tour, we stopped in Seattle and Anna's father Thomas showed up for the signing."

Grace practically choked on her mouthful of food. "Oh, how wonderful," she finally said. "How did Anna respond, or did she?"

"Well, I'll have to admit she was taken with him, holding out her arms for him to pick her up."

"So he acknowledged that he was the child's father?" Mark asked, as his wife frowned at him.

Maggie took a moment to respond. "He did, and we left it open for him to be a part of our lives in the future."

"Does Anna look at all like him?" Grace hurriedly asked.

"Yes, she seems to have his brown eyes and hair."

"So, how did the tour go?" Mark asked.

"Exhausting, but the ashram had alerted Ma hi' Ma's devotees, so there were plenty of them at every stop buying books and adding to the tour's success."

"Well, as they say, 'never look at gift horse in the mouth,'" her father added.

"So you took a nanny and she stayed back at the hotel with

Anna during the signings?" Grace asked.

"No, I brought her along, and they sat next to me." Grace looked at her daughter for a further explanation, but Maggie was still not ready to share her guru's prophesy with them, which is why the devotees showed up in such large numbers.

"Well, all my colleagues are impressed: a *New York Times* bestselling author. If we sell a thousand books, we're happy," Mark said without a twinge of jealousy.

The next morning everybody woke up early and converged on the Christmas tree to exchange presents. The gifts between Maggie and her parents were modest, but they showered their granddaughter with clothes and toys, almost to excess in Maggie's mind. Since it was their way of showing affection, she didn't say anything and was especially grateful for the new clothes. Anna was growing so fast that it was hard to keep up with her baby wardrobe given her modest income.

Mark took the family to their traditional Christmas brunch at a local restaurant where he had a standing holiday reservation. The owner, Max, was pleased with the new family addition —he remembered Maggie from years earlier—and asked if Jill and her family would be joining them.

"She's in Michigan with her in-laws," Mark said. Max set a table for three with a highchair for Anna.

When ordering for them, her father was pleased to learn that Maggie was now a lacto vegetarian and would eat eggs for breakfast. After the waitress left to retrieve their coffee order, Grace asked her daughter:

"Why the switch, if Anna is still a vegan?"

"I need the protein, and I tried feeding her cow's milk and eggs but she wouldn't touch them."

Mark frowned. "Well, shouldn't the mother determine her child's needs?"

Again Maggie waited to respond. "Well, in this case, I think my daughter knows what's best for her."

Mark shook his head in consternation. "Well, let's hope that dictum is not universally applied, or you're in for a rough ride with her."

Grace quickly changed the subject. "So, are you working on another book?"

"Yes, Mother. It's called *Heart Lines*, and it's about Lisa's heart connection with other children."

"Do you have a publication date?" her father asked.

"No, I just started it...wanted to see how *Lifelines* would sell first."

"So, how much money is there in bestselling children's books? I mean, can you support yourself with writing alone?"

Grace just sat back in her chair and shook her head. Her husband just didn't know when to let up and keep his mouth shut.

"I'm not expecting to. I think once Anna is older, I'll go back to teaching, but who knows what will happen. I never expected this windfall, so I don't know what else is in store for us."

Mark was about to say something, no doubt to comment about the futility of waiting for more windfalls, but held his tongue. Their breakfast was served, and they focused on eating their meal and returning to their house, expecting friends and neighbors to stop by for Christmas get-togethers.

Maggie dressed Anna in one of her new Christmas gift outfits, and as would be expected she was the focus of everybody's attention and goodwill, and given that she was older now, Maggie let people hold her. One neighbor in particular, an Hispanic woman, Marie Chavez, who appeared rather sickly— Maggie would later learn she had stomach cancer—held Anna for the longest time and refused to give her up.

"You know children's energies are so healing," Marie said, trying to explain her attachment to Anna. "It's why we place the cribs of babies in the old people's bedrooms at night, and your Anna's energy feels really wonderful." Maggie watched her as she spoke, and for the first time she could detect a person's aura and saw several red splotches in Marie's field starting to turn white. She couldn't wait to share this story with Ma hi' Ma, but wondered if Anna had healing abilities, in which this was seemingly its first manifestation, and what it might bring into their lives. Finally, Marie and her husband Jorge left. A month later, when Marie's cancer went into remission, she didn't associate it with her Christmas day visit to the Langfords.

When hearing the news, Grace did start to wonder about her granddaughter and Marie's claim about a baby's healing energy, and on their next visit would suggest that Anna's crib be moved into their bedroom at night.

Chapter 9

As Anna grew and her hand gestures were more expressive, it became clear to Maggie that she was communicating with spirit beings, or could at least detect their presence around her and would smile and wave her hands in the air at them. On trips to the park, Maggie was asked by more than one mother about Anna staring into space and waving her hands. She was not prepared to share her intuition about these episodes to complete strangers, and just said her daughter had a lot of energy and these hand gestures were just an expression of that. One woman replied, "Well, buy her Legos and puzzles when she gets older to keep her hands busy, before this becomes too disruptive."

While Maggie didn't want to interfere with her spiritually precocious child's spirit exchange, she also didn't want her daughter's behavior to draw too much undo attention to her. In the past she had just waited for her daughter to talk to her and hoped that she would sense her mother's discomfort and respond. But, as these episodes increased while shopping for groceries or just taking her out for a stroll down the street, Maggie impatiently waited for that contact. One day at home, while Anna was apparently telepathically conversing with the spirits in the house, she turned and stared at her mother. Maggie became very quiet, and again heard a voice in her head, but now she was able to respond telepathically:

"Why you concern? Is speaking with spirits not good?"

"It is good, but hand movements draw attention to you, and best you stop waving your hands in the air."

"Very well," Anna replied telepathically. She continued her exchange with the others in the room, but without gesturing. She followed through with this practice in public, and this behavior soon became a nonissue. But, it made Maggie think about her daughter's future spiritual development and how that would be increasingly hard to conceal from public scrutiny. It was spring, and while Maggie had told Gary Pritchard that she would visit Ma after the holiday season, the publicity duties of a bestselling author with its many radio interviews from home had delayed that trip. Now, as this telepathic exchange between Anna and her spirit guides grew to include her, Maggie thought it was time to pay Ma hi' Ma a visit. She wanted to explore her concerns about Anna's spiritual expression and how it might be perceived as disruptive by less-than-enlightened public health and school officials in the future.

Ma was delighted by the proposed visit, and she picked a weekend that would be unusually quiet at the ashram with few outside visitors. Maggie arrived on Friday afternoon. She was told to leave her car keys with Prema, who would move her luggage to their room, and she and her daughter were whisked away for an audience with Guru.

After Anna was situated on a pile of decorative pillows next to Guru, much to the child's delight, Maggie and Ma were served yogi tea. There was an exchange of pleasantries about Anna and then about the ashram and its news.

"So, Maggie," Ma said. "What's bothering you so much that you would take a trip to Northern California?"

Maggie composed herself. "Anna is apparently communicating with the spirits around her, and making hand gestures that have alarmed others." She paused, as Ma nodded her head.

"Doesn't sound like much of a problem to me," Ma added. "Tell them it's none of their business."

"But, while she is only a baby now, when she gets older, I'm concerned that her spiritually precocious behavior may draw attention to her and maybe even concern by health officials."

Ma considered this dilemma. "Of course, that would not be problem here in the ashram, but I understand your desire to remain...in the world." Her guru paused. "Have you asked Anna about this...telepathically?"

"She did ask me about my concern with her hand gestures, and I was finally able to have a conversation with her, and she modified them."

"May I?" Ma asked, turning to Anna who was watching the two of them closely.

"Of course." Maggie watched as Ma focused on Anna and the child on her. After a minute or two, Ma said, "I'm not getting an exchange with her. You try."

Maggie turned to her daughter. *"We are concerned about how your spiritual life may draw unwanted attention to you."*

"I know. My guides say they will protect me always. But, do what you must."

"Thank you." Maggie turned to Ma and related the message.

"Well, I think we need to consult with James Edwards." Ma reached into her pocket and withdrew an iPhone. Maggie gawked at her. "Dear, you can't run a twenty-first century ministry with smoke signals." She punched out a number. "James, I'm here with Maggie Langford and her spiritually precocious Anna, and I have a question for you." Ma set down the phone and activated the speaker.

"What may that be?"

"Anna, as we've spoken about, is an advanced soul, a former Hindu Guru and Tibetan Rinpoche, and even as a baby, her... spiritual behavior has drawn attention to her."

"I see and understand Maggie's concern." There was a long pause. "There isn't much legal precedent for this, but the easiest and simplest solution is to make Anna, at an appropriate but early age, a recognized guru or priest in a spiritual tradition such as your Hindu line. This way her 'spiritual expression' is protected by religious freedom."

Ma looked at Maggie who was considering this proposal. "Would this need to be made public?" Maggie asked.

"Well, just within the Hindu spiritual community, but we would need the appropriate authentications to show any wary health officials later on."

"And if she starts talking to Krishna on the playground, this would protect her from their inquiries?"

"Any inquiries about such behavior can be deflected by her religious status, but I would recommend homeschooling and a marshalling of her contact with the general public until she is old enough to consider these concerns and adjust her behavior."

"Thank you, Mr. Edwards. I'll take this under advisement."

"James," Ma added, "I'll speak to you about this later. Thank you for your time."

"I am always available to you, Ma. You know that."

Ma disconnected the phone call, and turned to Maggie who was still considering the implications of this suggestion.

"I know you don't want to…specialize Anna—I think that is the word you've used—but with 'lions be a jackal,' and it's best to prepare for this kind of scrutiny."

Maggie nodded her head. "Yes, Ma. The reason for my visit."

"Okay, so that's taken care of…or for now. I'll let you return to your room and freshen up, and we'll meet for dinner. I believe they are preparing a banquet of sorts, but nothing too elaborate or specific to Anna."

Maggie stood and picked up Anna. "Thank you, Ma. We look forward to it."

The remainder of the visit was very pleasant, and the devotees knew not to treat Anna with any special attention, but it was obvious that her energy like their guru's affected those open to it. Driving home Sunday afternoon, Maggie had to give Edwards's suggestion some serious consideration. Again it was exactly the kind of spiritual status bestowed on young Krishnamurti that she was trying to avoid, but she also didn't want to get into pitch battles with health officials over Anna's mental condition. Maggie got a partial answer when they pulled into a restaurant in Monterey on the long drive home. Anna was seated in her high chair and staring into space off to the side, no doubt in communication with ethereal beings, while everybody else was looking out the windows at the churning ocean. A woman walking past them carrying a tray stopped and stared at Anna for a long moment, before somebody "accidently" knocked into her tray and spilled her soft drink onto the floor. This drew her attention back to the accident and the clumsy teenager who had caused it. Maggie was watching the whole scene develop, when she turned and looked back at Anna who was smiling at her. She got the message: her daughter was protected. Maggie also realized that her guides would need to be made aware of such "problems" to address them earlier than later in Anna's development.

Chapter 10

Now being able to initiate telepathic communication with her daughter allowed Maggie to express her safety concerns as they arose for the most part. While Anna no longer waved to invisible friends in public, Maggie's silent telepathic exchanges with her in grocery stores or on walks through the park did draw some attention. Most just figured Maggie was giving her child stern looks to discipline her behavior, but this was San Luis Obispo, a West Coast spiritual hotspot, and there were metaphysical practitioners here who suspected more was happening. While the local Ma devotees were sworn to secrecy by their guru, it was hard to contain such rumors. When Anna was old enough to play with the local children at the park, Maggie noticed that she was very hands-on with her friends, or those with runny noses or colds, which soon cleared up. Maggie asked her daughter if she were healing them, and she confirmed her mother's suspicions. For the most part, this went unnoticed by the other mothers at the park or at the yoga center playroom where Anna stayed when her mother attended classes.

Maggie picked up and started to reread her copy of *The Autobiography of a Yogi*, because she remembered Yogananda addressing these concerns with his devotees: when do you interfere with someone's karma by healing them. She also read that Anandamayi Ma only healed people when prompted by Spirit. Maggie didn't want to run back to the ashram and question Ma hi' Ma every time such an issue arose and trusted that it would work itself out. The first real challenge arose when a sickly little boy, Martin, appeared at the park that summer — his head was shaved and Maggie figured he had cancer and was taking chemotherapy. Anna's first impulse was to be taken over to him, but Maggie denied her request.

Anna questioned her mother, *"I not to heal him?"*

Maggie was differently conflicted. *"For today, let us avoid contact with him."*

"As you wish, Mother."

That night after dinner, Maggie placed her daughter on the living room rug but in eyesight of her while she washed the dinner dishes. She noticed that Anna had gone into one of her swaying trance states, and Maggie finished up and stepped over to the sofa to watch her. The sacred energy generated by these states suffused the house and Maggie just naturally went into a meditation. After a while she felt a shift as her spirit left her body, and she found herself in an altered spiritual dimension or space, a park-like daylight setting with a natural spring. Across from her she saw her daughter, somewhat older in her spirit body, sitting there with a man in a gleaming white suit whose saintly aura was quite pronounced. They were dangling their feet in the pool of spring water. Anna waved her mother over.

Maggie stepped over and sat across from them and dipped her bare feet into the water.

"Joseph tells me you right, that just healing the boy is…"

"A complicated issue," Joseph said. "Sometimes souls, especially children, pick sickly bodies to work out their karma from past lives."

She nodded her head. Maggie was tempted to ask him who he was, but figured he would tell her when it was appropriate. "So, how does one know?"

Anna smiled, shaking her head as if Maggie should've known the answer. "You ask their soul, or their spirit."

"And if his soul says yes, and Anna miraculously heals him and the word gets out, the infirm will start lining up at our door."

Joseph smiled. "We, her spirit guides, understand your concern. In such cases, Anna can remotely heal him or energize a bottle of water or a bite of food as the conduit."

"So you agree that Anna's Being needs to be…"

"Allowed its expression, but as her guardian parent your

concerns must be honored." He paused and then smiled. "We of the spirit world are not always the best judge of how humans will react to Spirit and its manifestations."

The scene dissolved, and she found herself back in the apartment with Anna sitting in her playpen smiling at her mother.

"I asked Martin's spirit, and he said he not ready yet, but maybe one day soon."

"Thank Joseph for me."

"He says the three of us have been together in other lives and that this will be grand adventure."

Maggie smiled at her daughter, went over and picked her up, and walked back to Anna's room and put her to sleep. In her office, she felt inspired to work on her book *Heart Lines*, and always wrote or drew pictures after intense spiritual contact with Anna, treating her daughter as a kind of inspirational collaborator. She now understood that *Lisa's Lifelines* was not only inspired by how Anna interacted with others, even as a child, but Maggie suspected that there may have been dreamtime exchanges that she did not recall. As Joseph said, this would be a grand adventure...together.

Over the next six months Anna learned to walk ahead of schedule and began to speak a few words—Kris was one of the first she uttered, and Maggie assumed it was short for Krishna. Since Maggie had made only one more visit to the ashram, where Anna might have heard the Hindu god's name spoken, Maggie assumed it was a spirit contact and left it at that. She had been around enough manifestation of spiritual ego at the ashram not to project too much onto such displays; she knew her daughter was a highly evolved soul but didn't consider it further. Keeping others disinformed and deflecting their own projection was more difficult. This became a challenge when her mother, Grace, had a health crisis: she was discovered to have breast cancer, and upon hearing this news, Maggie packed up her daughter and they drove down to be with her mother while she was considering her medical options.

It appeared that as soon as Anna saw her grandmother that some part of her knew her condition immediately, as if she could almost see the cancerous cells spreading in her breasts. Maggie gave her daughter a look before she toddled over and let her grandmother hug her. That afternoon, as Maggie was putting her daughter down for a nap, they had an exchange:

"I ask and her spirit said it is allowed."

"Okay," Maggie thought. *"But I want to be careful about her healing, not to let her figure it out."*

Then Maggie heard Joseph's voice in her head, *"Let her carry Anna on her chest."*

"Of course, we'll use my flip carrier. Thank you, Joseph."

And so that afternoon, Maggie and her mother went for a walk on the beach, and she fitted Grace with Anna's flip carrier. While Anna was facing forward, Maggie figured the long physical contact was enough to transfer the needed energy and healing. After a while Grace remarked how warm she felt, and they found a bench to sit on.

"I can take Anna, if she is too much of a strain," Maggie said.

"Oh no. I'm fine. I just feel flushed, but a good flush. Just give me a minute."

Maggie then added. "Mother, I know you're wedded to your doctor, but maybe you should get a second opinion."

Grace looked at her daughter about to protest when Anna became particularly animated. "So, I take it that this is a family request," Grace added, looking at her granddaughter suspiciously.

Maggie shrugged her shoulders and tried to deflect her mother's inquiry. "Oh, you mean Anna's activity." She pointed out the seagulls flying nearby. "It's the seagulls, Mom. Nothing more, really."

Grace stood up. "Well, I kind of like this flush feeling, so let's keep walking, dear."

Three weeks later, Grace called Maggie to inform her that a second PET scan didn't show any cancer growth. "My doctor compared the film and can't understand how the machine could have malfunctioned, but I told him to let it go."

"That's wonderful news, Mom," Maggie said, trying to sound surprised.

"Well, thank Anna for me," her mother said. "Maybe Marie was right about babies' energies."

"I'm sure it was more than that, Mom," Maggie said.

Her mother wasn't willing to press the issue, and she was grateful. Maggie only hoped that her father, whose spirit might decline Anna's help, would take better care of his health. But, she figured more physical contact between him and her daughter on their now more frequent visits might be a kind of preventative medicine measure for him, and made a note to question Joseph about it next time he popped up in their lives.

Chapter 11

In the fall Maggie's second book, *Lisa's Heart Lines*, was published to both critical and popular success. This time she felt more comfortable leaving Anna with her parents while she went on another two-week book tour. She had a "talk" with her daughter while driving down to Santa Barbara, and even had a word with Joseph, and they both assured her that the child Anna would "behave" herself, spiritually speaking. While she called her mother nearly every day from the road, Maggie was on alert when the three of them picked her up at the airport—she had started her tour with a book signing at Chaucer's, left her car with her parents, and flew out from Santa Barbara. It was obvious that they had a secret but were waiting to tell Maggie, and they were almost home when Anna finally blurted out, "Dog."

Maggie looked at her mother in the front passenger's seat, but she only smiled back. At the house she found a golden retriever tied up in the front yard. "Whose dog is that?"

Her father shook his head and her mother only smiled again. When Maggie opened the door, Anna squirmed out of her arms and ran over to the two-year-old dog who lay down on the grass and allowed Anna to crawl all over him.

"Okay. What's up, Mom?"

"Well, it seemed like every dog in the neighborhood was finding its way over here to play with Anna, and Mark knew a breeder of purebred retrievers, and..."

"Don't tell me you bought a dog for her?"

"Well, we got him on loan to see how you'd like him."

Maggie shook her head. "Mom, my place is too small for a big dog and besides..." But she only had to look at Anna, her hands wrapped around his neck, the dog licking her face, to know this was a hopeless battle.

Maggie stepped over and sat down on the lawn next to him. "What's his name?"

"Well, you're not going to believe this, but one of the reasons we picked him or got one at all was because of his name," Grace said in self-defense. Maggie looked back at her expectantly. "Bodhi...short for Bodhisattva."

"You're kidding?"

Mark volunteered, "Yeah, Barry's a screenwriter of sorts and was a friend of Patrick Swayze, and named him after his character in the surfing movie *Point Break*."

Maggie petted the dog who turned and put his head in her lap, and she just melted. She turned to her daughter. "Well, my apartment allows dogs, so I guess we'll give it a try."

Anna jumped up and gave her a big hug, wrapping her arms around her mother's legs. Grace had watched this exchange while Mark unloaded Maggie's luggage. "How did she understand that?"

"Body language, Mom. Body language."

After spending two weeks with her granddaughter, who had the most extraordinary effect on people and animals and after her own miraculous recovery from cancer, Grace was officially suspicious of Anna's apparent premature cognition and her healing effect on those around her.

When they arrived home and took a stroll through the park that first night, it became obvious to Maggie that Anna was in telepathic contact with Bodhi. At one point he squatted on the lawn to "do his business," when Anna stared at him, and he stood up on all fours and ran into the bushes.

"Did you tell Bodhi do that, Anna?"

"Yes, Mama," Anna replied. *"Is not better?"*

"Well, for now. I'll put baggies in the stroller for next time."

Maggie wondered if she could talk with Bodhi herself, but decided not to test that idea quite yet. It was one thing to "talk" with her evolved daughter, but communicating with a dog was quite another. However, she picked up the book, *The Dog Whisperer*, and began to read it. At some point she realized that Bodhi was on a kind of protection detail: He would never leave Anna's side, slept in her room, and watched her like a secret service agent wherever they went. One of the mothers at the park noted how attentive Bodhi was, and asked Maggie if he had been trained as a guard dog.

"Well, not formally. But he kind of acts that way."

"Have you noticed the eye contact between them?" the woman asked. "It's as if they're communicating with each other."

"Evelyn, you're getting carried away. Anna's just particularly attached to him." The woman shook her head and walked off. Maggie made a note to "talk" with Anna about this overt behavior with her dog, but for now at least she felt more relaxed and less on guard while Anna was out in public. She knew Bodhi was there helping her watch over her daughter.

As Anna approached her second birthday, Maggie was concerned that she didn't speak as many words as other children her age. She read that by age two she should be saying as many as forty or fifty words, when Anna only spoke twenty or so. Maggie knew it wasn't a developmental problem, and she asked the child's being.

"You're not speaking as well as you should."

"Why speak when we can mind talk?"

"Because you won't be able to speak with others later."

Anna thought about this for a moment, and then said out loud, "Yes, Mama."

From that point Anna made more of an effort to pick up language, but it was clear to Maggie that as time went on she would never have as developed a social life as she apparently enjoyed with a host of inner beings. This was a concern of Maggie's. At this point Anna formally meditated and even crossed her little legs in the *lotus* position for hours at a time. While she could appreciate her child's inner life, she wanted her to balance that with an outer focus. So, she started taking Anna out of the house on more walks to the park and to the beach, trips to the store, and especially to yoga class.

The latter turned into another demonstration of Anna's accelerated development. One day, while Maggie and her class were doing simple asanas on their mats, Anna found a small mat and joined her mother. Her yoga teacher, Riva, indulged the child, expecting her to collapse into a ball of arms and legs. But, when Anna did most of the asanas fairly well, the teacher was taken aback.

"Maggie, have you been teaching her at home?"

"No. Like with meditation, it must be a past-life thing."

"Well, let's start to include Anna as a student and we'll see how much she can do."

"Fine. As long as you don't bring TV crews in to film your prodigy."

Riva laughed. "And why would that be a problem? Promoting child yoga seems advantageous."

"There are other issues, and I don't feel like I need to defend my decision."

Riva nodded her head. "Okay. For now it's a private thing, but a two-year-old yogi is certainly going to draw some attention."

Maggie smiled and laid back on her mat in the *Shavasana* or resting pose, and Anna followed her mother's lead. After class they returned her borrowed mat, and Maggie bought Anna her own mat. Afterward they walked down the block to the Bliss Café. As they walked inside, Anna said, "Yogi tea."

"Very good, Anna," Maggie said encouragingly.

She ordered two and treated Anna to the "Little Yogi Bowl" of rice, beans, and chutney. It was intended for older children, but the name seemed appropriate to the occasion, and she could always finish what Anna couldn't eat. She ate a power salad herself and allowed Anna to pick items from it.

After finishing half of the rice bowl, Anna sat back and

watched her mother.

"You're upset, me doing yoga?"

Maggie looked around to make sure they weren't being monitored. *"No. Just concerned about the reaction of others."*

Anna nodded her head. She closed her eyes as if hearing an inner voice. "Bodhi, pee-pee walk."

Maggie took money out of her purse and laid it on the table. "Let's hurry. We don't want to keep him waiting." As they walked to her car, Maggie realized that Anna's telepathy did have some practical applications, and recalling a recent walk in the woods, wondered if she were prescient as well. They had come to a forked path and Anna steered them to the right. After walking twenty yards or so, Maggie heard and then saw through the sparse foliage a jogger and his two big dogs tromping down the left-side path. She looked down at her daughter but she just continued walking with a smile and petting Bodhi to calm him down. Of course Maggie had seen overblown movies about child psychics, which only reinforced her natural inclination to marshal Anna's contacts with the outside world, or until which time she could discipline the display of her *siddhis*, or powers, as they were called in the Eastern world.

Chapter 12

After the success of her first two books, in which her illustrations won several awards, Maggie branched out into illustrating children's books for her publisher and others. Combined with the royalties from her own books, this allowed Maggie to support her and Anna without having to work a day job or go back to teaching. Thus the two of them led a fairly cloistered life, which suited her daughter's temperament just fine. In fact, Anna now spent hours each day in ecstatic trance states, and when she wasn't meditating, she drew pictures. Apparently she had inherited her mother's artistic talent and would draw pictures of her spirit friends, at first in crayons and then with colored pencils, that were quite elaborate. Upon seeing them, friends encouraged Maggie to put them on display at art festivals, but she didn't want to draw any further attention to her daughter's talents.

Anna's only real contact with other children was at the park, since she no longer stayed in the yoga studio's daycare center and practiced with the adults. While the apartment complex had a playground, Anna preferred to stay at home and didn't interact much with the children there. Maggie couldn't imagine that this would cause a problem, but apparently one of the mothers there began to worry about Anna's cloistered existence and wondered if she was being unnaturally constrained by her reclusive mother. This led her to report the situation to the county's Child Services.

Maggie answered the door one afternoon to be greeted by a black middle-aged woman in a business suit. "How can I help you?"

"Are you Margret Langford?"

"Yes, I am."

She looked down at a sheet of paper. "The mother of Anna

Langford, age four?"

"Yes. What is this about?"

The woman stuck out her hand, which Maggie shook. "I'm Beverly Foster from Child Services. May I come in and talk with you?"

Maggie was taken aback but opened the door and allowed the woman to step inside. She followed Maggie into the living room and took a seat across from her as Maggie sat on the sofa.

"Is Anna home?" Beverly asked.

"Ms. Foster, please tell me why you're here," Maggie insisted.

"Well, don't be alarmed, but one of the mothers here at the apartment complex has reported that you child is unusually reclusive. We just wanted to check to see if there was a health or emotional issue that we could help with."

Maggie took a deep breath and tried to calm herself and not overreact. "Anna has an…artistic temperament." Maggie pointed out several of her daughter's drawings that were framed and hung on the living room walls. "As you can see, she's quite a budding artist and as such has a very active interior life."

Ms. Foster stood up and took a closer look at the pictures. "They are all of angels or spirits, and no drawings of people, pets, or something in nature. Is that healthy?"

"Read any of a number of books on the spiritual life of children and you'll find this is quite normal, if precocious."

The woman nodded her head. "Could I see Anna, maybe look into her bedroom?"

"Please have a seat, and I'll check on her."

"I'd prefer to go in unannounced," the woman insisted.

Maggie again calmed herself. "It'll just be a minute. Stand here." She walked down the hall and knocked on Anna's door. "Dear, may I come in?" She opened the door and had a look-see. Anna was sitting on the floor drawing—she wasn't meditating or in a trance state as Maggie had feared—and Bodhi was lying on the floor beside her. She and Anna exchanged looks. The child put down her pencil.

Maggie waved Ms. Foster over, and the two of them stepped into Anna's room. Bodhi immediately stood up and placed himself between the stranger and Anna.

"Anna, tell Bodhi to sit down." After a moment, Bodhi sauntered over to the corner of the room and lay down.

"Anna, this nice lady is Beverly Foster, and she wanted to say hello to you."

Beverly stepped over and squatted down on her haunches. "Anna, you are quite the artist."

Anna smiled winningly. "I like to draw."

"I can see that. What else do you like to do?"

"I like to pray, go to the park and beach."

"What about playing with other children? Do you like to do that?"

"Sometimes, but they slow."

"Maybe you should give them more of a chance," Foster added.

Anna smiled winningly. "Maybe."

She stood up. "It was certainly nice to meet you, Anna."

"I like you too," Anna said, and went back to drawing her angel picture.

Maggie and Beverly went back to the living room where the woman picked up her purse. "Well, she seems well-adjusted, if introverted, and fairly advanced for her age. I would suggest more contact with other children, but otherwise I see no problem here and that's what my report will say. Thank you for allowing me to visit with both of you."

It was only after she left the apartment and was driving to her next appointment that it struck Beverly that in the bedroom the little girl had not verbally instructed her dog to sit down. How did he know to do that? Also, this was the first time she ever heard a child her age say she liked to pray. Beverly filed a report clearing the issue, but later she decided to add a personal note to herself to do a follow-up visit in a year's time. She would also check to see if they were receiving child support from the father, since Margret Langford's file listed her as a single mother. This note was somehow misplaced and she didn't do a follow-up visit as planned.

After her mother and the woman with the dark cloud around her left, Anna put down her colored pencil, went over to her meditation pillow and sat. She could sense the woman's concern and her mother's own fearful reaction to her and to the threat she presented. This confused her. Anna operated at such a high level of trust with her spirit guides, the Divine, and even with Bodhi and her mother that this fear, or so she had heard her mother describe it, was strange to her. Did these adults not know that everything happens in the divinely orchestrated play between all levels of existence, or so she sensed? She would not yet articulate it in these terms, but her spirit informed her of this in its own nonverbal way. But, she was slowly coming to realize or sense that it was this mental language expression in itself that was the root of the problem for them.

The more she spoke and used language and listened to adult speech patterns, she could sense or feel something developing inside of her, a kind of social or mental self that grew with her use of language. She had asked Joseph, and he said it was normal but not to confuse her real self with it, like everyone here eventually does. She asked, why allow it? He told her that it was the basis for humanity's communal interchange and one's ability to communicate with others. He also reminded her that the divine included everything and she was, as the saying goes, a spiritual being having a human experience. Anna liked this concept, and it made her feel more at ease about allowing her talky self, as she liked to refer to it, a freer reign. She now could sense her mother's bad feelings, and she stood up and walked out to the living room.

"Time for walk," she said as a statement and not a question.

Maggie turned to her daughter and stared at her for a moment. "Yes, dear. Let's do a beach walk.

Anna's eyes lit up. "Goody, mama." Anna looked at Bodhi and he barked and ran to the door.

Maggie bundled Anna up in her winter coat and gloves, grabbed her own coat and the dog's leash, and they walked out the door. They drove down to Pismo Beach. On the way there, Anna asked, "Why you 'fraid of woman?"

"Not afraid, just cautious," Maggie replied, glancing into the rearview mirror at her daughter in her front-forward car seat.

"She want to harm me?"

"No, dear. Nobody wants to harm you, but some people don't understand how Spirit works and want to help out in their own muddled way."

"Sometimes, you don't, Mommy."

"I need to trust more?" Maggie asked.

"Yes," Anna said, and then switched the subject. "We get mustard...thing?"

"Pretzels," Maggie clarified, smiling at her daughter.

"Everything good. You see."

It was low tide, and the walk along the shore did wonders for Maggie's mood, and afterward they headed back to the boardwalk and its concession stands. She bought each of them, including Bodhi, a pretzel—his without mustard—and hot chocolate for her and Anna.

The two of them sat at a booth inside the restaurant and looked out at the ocean. After they became mesmerized by this churning wave action for a while, Anna turned to her mother. "We live on ocean sometime..."

"It is very expensive here," Maggie added.

Anna shook her head. "Wish and trust, Mommy. Everything yours."

"I'll keep that in mind, dear."

On the way out, she picked up *The Tribune* newspaper, and saw the front page article on the arrival in town of a bestselling author, who was giving a lecture and signing books at Barnes and Noble on Wednesday. Driving back to their apartment, Maggie started to think about writing a third children's book. She had a tendency of being satisfied that all their needs were being met, but didn't give any thought to the future or how more income could make their life easier. She wondered if Anna had set the stage for this endeavor with her wanting to live closer to the ocean. Well, she thought, Santa Barbara would make that a reality, but did she want to live that close to her parents?

Chapter 13

After the visit from Child Services, Maggie was tempted to take James Edwards's advice and eventually have Anna initiated as a Hindu guru. She made further inquiries of Ma hi' Ma at the next *Maha Shivaratri* festival the following March. Now that Anna was older she could more easily handle the "heightened atmosphere" at the ashram. Her guru was open to the idea, but insisted that she and Anna move to the ashram for a year in order for her to instruct the child further. While Maggie and her daughter sat on pillows in the temple room and she discussed this matter with Guru, Anna shook her head at one point.

"You object, child?" Ma asked.

"Not want to be guru, or live here."

"And why is that?" Ma inquired further. Maggie was about to intercede, but Guru raised a hand to quiet her.

"Joseph says better I be out in world now."

"Joseph?" Ma asked, looking questioningly at Maggie.

"A spirit guide, he says. You want to meet?" Anna asked.

Ma smiled indulgently. "Yes. Very much so."

Anna made a swirling upward motion with her right hand, and the three of them, or their spirit bodies, were suddenly transported to the spring where Joseph sat on a bench with Anna. Maggie and Ma sat across from them.

Joseph wore a white suit of sorts, his gray hair lustrous in the preternatural light.

"How interesting," Ma said, somewhat in shock, looking at Maggie who just smiled.

"Ma, nice of you to join us. We are appreciative of your spiritual oversight of young Anna."

"We?" Ma asked timidly, somewhat in awe of the man.

Joseph smiled. "Anna's spiritual guides."

"Who would prefer that she remain outside of any one

tradition?"

"Yes, we have decided in consort with her Spirit that she not be initiated as suggested, or at least for now. There may come a time when it's...necessary." This caught Maggie's attention. What did he mean by that, she wondered.

Before she could inquire further, Joseph addressed Ma's apparent confusion. "This does not preclude her further instruction in Hinduism and your own guidance of her in that faith."

"I see. And the issue of her religious expression?"

"We will protect her from those, unlike yourself, who would exploit or stifle her."

"I understand and will concur."

Anna smiled at Joseph. "I tell you she very good guru."

Joseph just smiled back, twirled his hand, as the scene dissolved and the three of them were again in the ashram's temple room.

Ma was still a little unnerved by this intercession, as it were. She turned to Maggie. "This has happened before?"

"Yes, Ma. There was a question about Anna's healings, and Joseph clarified the issue for us."

Ma finally chuckled to herself. "Well, how can one disagree with the child's own spirit guide?" She turned and looked at Anna. "So be it, or for now. But, as Joseph kindly emphasized, your own religious instruction will follow soon."

"Yes, Ma," Anna said and bowed her head. Reassured of her place in the child's celestial pecking order, Ma dismissed Anna and her mother and slipped into a meditative state to further align her will with God's and that of her emissaries.

Ma gave Maggie several Hindu children's books of myths and stories to take back with her and to use as Anna's initial reading material. This, however, created a problem—not the material per se, but the child's resistance to reading.

While Anna was a little young to begin reading, Maggie

was acquiring a broader elementary school teaching degree, if through correspondence and Internet courses, and was qualified to teach reading, but her daughter resisted.

"Me not want to learn read yet," she insisted after her mother's initial instruction.

"It will open new worlds to you, dear," her mother insisted.

"And close others," Anna insisted. The child crossed her legs and went into a meditative trance state, and she would not discipline her further at this time. Maggie left Anna to her own devices and went back to her bedroom and lay down. She found that any conflict with her daughter was very tiring, and the best recourse was to take a nap. Maggie fell asleep almost instantly and found herself back in the park with Joseph, but just with just the two of them this time.

"I've been meaning to consult with you about this," Joseph said sheepishly, as if he had been neglectful of his duties.

"About Anna learning to read early?"

"Yes. It's a delicate balance. She must further shore up, I believe the term is, her connection to her Self, or what you would call her Higher Self, before reading and mental activity develops the ego self, as you would say, much further."

"I see. Thank you for that clarification."

"As always we are...appreciative of your guidance of her as well."

Maggie woke from the nap to find Anna lying beside her. She rolled over and looked at her daughter. "You went without me," she said almost accusingly.

"Didn't mean to, dear. But Joseph summoned me."

Anna nodded her head and smiled. "Hurt, I was," she said with a self-depreciating smile. "You have your own spirit life, need to...allow."

Bodhi walked into the room as if on cue. "Time for walk," Maggie said to him, and he barked. Anna looked at her mother. "Bodhi need bath soon."

"We'll take him to *All Paws* Saturday."

"Me want to wash him," Anna said in a pout.

"I'm sure they'll let you, dear."

They got ready to head out. It was early April and the weather had turned warm, and all they needed were light coats. At the park, as Bodhi ran free and stretched his legs, Maggie and Anna found Martin's mother sitting on a park bench crying. She stepped over and sat down next to her and learned that her son Martin was in the hospital dying.

Anna immediately added, "We go see him."

Dorothy looked at Anna and smiled. "He would like that. Visiting hours start at seven, but he's in intensive care and I'm not sure how close you can get to him."

On the drive to the Sierra Vista hospital that night, Maggie asked her daughter, "Did you check with his Spirit?"

"Yes, Mama. He ready be healed. Had enough pain, he tell me."

"Okay, but let's do this in stages. Tonight and then in another day or so, but not too fast or too obvious."

"Not control. I send energy. It does what it does."

Maggie was a little alarmed that her daughter's visit would be connected to the boy's recovery, but she also realized that a boy's life was at stake and that she needed to trust Anna's guides to protect her from any unwanted scrutiny.

Apparently Anna's spirit had already initiated her healing work starting at the park, because by the time they arrived at the hospital that night, Martin had recovered to the point that he could see visitors. Anna held his hand the whole time, and while Maggie looked for any sudden changes, nothing obvious transpired. Dorothy thanked them for coming, and was a little amazed herself by her son's partial recovery, or his stepping back from the brink of death today.

The next night Maggie had asked if Anna wanted to return to the hospital, and she said that there was no need to. "Not like that place. Too much bad energy, but people nice. They try."

"And Martin?"

"We see him at park in summer."

As it happened and as the newspaper article recorded, Martin was miraculously healed of his Stage Four bone cancer. It was a gradual process over several months, and apparently there was no connecting link to Anna's visit, or so Maggie thought. That summer, as Martin played with Anna and Bodhi in the park, his mother sat next to Maggie.

"Thank you," she said.

"Oh, for the visit?" Maggie asked. "I wanted to go back, but Anna doesn't like hospitals."

"Me either, and not for the visit. I know what happened. I had asked the nurses, and they said Martin started to recover in the early afternoon, right after I told you and Anna about his condition, or so it seems."

Maggie was about to call her suspicions a "coincidence," but the woman shook her off. "I've heard the rumors about Anna, but won't say anything." Dorothy teared up. "Martin's fourth birthday is next week, and my husband and I would like you to join us."

Maggie gave the woman a questioning look. "No. He doesn't suspect a thing. Anna is his only real friend. The illness has cut him off from other children."

"We'd be glad to."

"And Martin wants you to bring Bodhi. We have a big backyard."

This episode more than anything else reassured Maggie that Anna's preternatural state of being and its expression did not require her constant monitoring. It was somewhat of a relief, and she could focus more energy on herself. Celebrating Martin's birthday with his family made it obvious to her that it was important that Anna spent some time with her father, and maybe with the three of them together, and so she wrote Thomas a letter hoping that he would agree to visit them. She had heard at the ashram that he was back from India on a teaching hiatus. She had to admit to herself that this inquiry was as much for her as it was for Anna. She was feeling the lack of a loving male connection in her life, and while she said her spiritual journey with Anna took precedence, its essence was love and she needed to open her heart to such a relationship. Maybe a brief loving exchange with Thomas would set the stage for something more lasting, but she sensed that like Anna her own journey was being orchestrated by her God Self and she just needed to "let go, and let God."

Chapter 14

After accepting Maggie's invitation, Thomas arrived in town six weeks later. He had arranged to teach several Kundalini Yoga classes in exchange for room and board at the Yoga Center. They had a room for visiting yogis and a kitchen used by the staff and students. Maggie allowed him to settle in, and the next day she and Anna picked Thomas up at the Center and took him to lunch at the nearby Bliss Café. They were able to walk there, and Anna held her father's hand all the way. Before Maggie extended her invitation, she had talked with Anna figuring she didn't remember Thomas from the book signing in Seattle. But, Anna said that she knew of him and often visited him in her dream state.

"He better yogi than our teacher."

"Well, we'll have to attend one of his classes."

"You make another baby? I want brother."

"Anna. Do not talk of this. We are only friends, but he is your father and you should get to know him."

Anna picked out her favorite outfit, and at lunch she was on her best behavior. She apparently wanted to impress Thomas, but he was already totally taken with her.

"Do you remember dream where we walk on beach?"

Thomas gazed at her daughter. "No, Anna. But I'm sure I enjoyed it."

"We have beach here. You take me for walk?"

"I'd love to, dear."

The waitress came and they began to order, but Anna interrupted the process. "You need more pro...tein."

Thomas laughed, and ordered extra tofu with his salad. While he wanted to talk with Maggie, Anna demanded his complete attention and they just allowed her to take center stage. Afterward they drove to Pismo Beach, and Maggie watched

Thomas and Anna walk on the beach with Bodhi while she sat on the pier. She was happy that her daughter had established a good relationship with her father, but she was concerned that once he left town it would greatly affect her. When they came back from their walk, the three of them went inside the surfside restaurant and ordered hot chocolates. Bodhi sat on the deck.

Thomas turned to Maggie. "I was amazed to hear that Anna has been doing Hatha Yoga with you and your class."

"Yes. She's quite the yogi, but she says that you're a better teacher than Vivian."

"She told me that, and I tried to explain that different types of yoga require different approaches, and it may only seem that way."

"We find out. Mama say we go to class."

"There's one tonight, and you're definitely invited," Thomas said. "Maybe afterward, I can drive over to your place and mommy and I can talk."

"You mean after Miss Take-Up-All-Your-Time has gone to bed."

Anna pretended to be mad and made a face, but couldn't keep up the pretense and burst out laughing. She turned to Thomas. "Me watch in spirit."

Thomas looked at them in amazement. "Yes, and if you have any health complaints, she's your girl," Maggie added.

That night after class, Maggie cooked them a late dinner. While she prepared it, Thomas and Anna walked Bodhi. After dinner and after Anna had been put to bed, Thomas and Maggie sat in the living room. "I told Swami Vinanda about Anna, or I just had to mention her name and he chimed in. Said she was a very advanced soul, and that you would have to bring her to India to visit her homeland, or where she had lived in many previous lifetimes."

Maggie smiled. "You don't say."

"Just passing along the suggestion."

"So, are you finished with this round of instruction, or do you go back soon?"

Thomas stared at Maggie for a long moment. "I teach at Swami V's ashram, and I had planned on returning in May, but being with Anna certainly makes that harder."

They just looked at each other and let this sentiment settle. "I can imagine. She's quite taken with you as well."

"So, where does that leave us?"

Maggie laughed. "You mean where does that leave you and Anna, since we haven't really established a relationship?"

"And if I were to stay in town, or moved to Ma hi' Ma's Ashram, and start to visit more often?"

"I think if you were to stay on this visit for a couple weeks, we'd be able to figure that out, or get a better handle on it."

"Of course. I'll ask at the Center, see if I can extend my stay. My sister lent me her second car, but I'm sure she'll let me keep it a while longer."

"Good." Maggie stood up and walked Thomas to the door. They hugged, but did not kiss.

"I'll call tomorrow and let you know how it goes with the studio."

When Maggie went to bed, she half expected a dreamtime visit by Joseph giving her relationship counseling, but she had no such encounter, or did not recall it, and was relieved. She was still attracted to Thomas, and she couldn't imagine being with any man who wasn't totally committed to self-realization, as he was. But, and maybe it just her new heightened sensitivity, he seemed much the same as before, or a bit immature. She knew a lot of spiritual men were what Carl Jung called *Puer Aeternus*, or the eternal boy who won't or can't integrate their feeling side. Some contemporaries called it the Peter Pan Syndrome. What was interesting in this regard was that Anna, as young as she was, defined spirituality in a much different light for her. Despite her trance states and long meditations, there was something very solid and grounded about Anna, which may be due to her perpetually stilled mind and the lack of any monkey-mind chatter. This beingness was what she hoped to achieve by dedicated meditation and mindfulness exercises, but wondered whether or how soon Thomas would take to such an accelerated integration himself.

In the morning Anna had crawled into her bed, as was often the case, and they had some girl time together. "Is daddy going away?"

"Anna, this was just a visit, but he's staying longer to spend more time with you."

"I not want him to go."

"We get that, dear. But, let's see how it all works out." Maggie paused, scooting up in bed so as to look her daughter in the eye. "Anna, Thomas has his own spiritual path, and you can't...hold him here for your own benefit."

"You want me let go of cords?"

Maggie stared at her daughter for a long moment. She thought that she heard her correctly, but wasn't quite sure. "You mean the energy cords that naturally form between people with emotional attachments?"

"Yes...and no."

"Anna," her mother said with emphasis.

She turned her head away. "I hold on to him with my... energy."

"We all do that with people we care about, but your energy is very...strong, and you must be careful and let people go so they can do what's best for them."

"Even if it not good for you?"

"Holding people against their will is never good for anybody."

"Okay." Her eyes teared up—the first time Maggie had ever seen her sad. "It'll be fine, Anna. You're see. Sometimes people choose what you want on their own without...help."

At Thomas's next yoga class, Maggie saw that the word

had gotten out about the young sexy instructor, and the yoga bunnies were lined up to attend his class. While Anna still took up a lot of his attention, it was obvious to her that Thomas was equally open to the adulation and sexual come-ons of the young female students. She knew that this was always the test for gurus-in-the-making, and how many exploited both women and men for sexual favors. In this case, it was also a test of their relationship possibilities. Maggie decided to allow Thomas more space and declined to go for coffee after class with him and the others. Anna didn't resist; apparently she didn't want to share her father's attention with other women.

Over the next week, they went to dinner once and Thomas came over to their house for brunch on Sunday, but Maggie kept the relationship cordial and nonsexual. On his part Thomas was equally aloof, testing his own feelings for Maggie while totally taken with his daughter Anna. This came to a head the next week. One morning Anna crawled into bed with her mother, and was a little weepy.

"What's wrong, dear?" Maggie immediately asked.

"Daddy with other woman last night."

Maggie sat up in bed. "Anna, you must not spy on your father."

"But, I want him to stay."

"He can, or can visit, and be with another woman. His relationship with you is not affected, just mine."

"But we not be happy family together."

"No, not if he wants to be with other women."

It was a rainy morning and they just lay in bed and after a while fell back to sleep together. Maggie and Anna didn't attend Thomas's class that night, and afterward he came over to the house.

"I missed the two of you at class tonight," he told them as they sat in the living room and drank Chai.

"Well, neither of us is in good shape today," Maggie said and left it at that.

"What about this weekend? I thought we might go camping together."

Anna stared at her father. "Just us?" she asked, rather ingenuously. Maggie gave her a look.

Thomas saw that exchange. "Anna, isn't it time for bed?" he asked.

"If you read to me," she said to her father.

Maggie stood up. "Let me get her in bed, and you can read her a story."

Afterward Thomas slinked back into the living room shaking his head. "Anna told me. Guess it's hard for me to keep secrets from her."

"Well, I've warned her about monitoring people."

Thomas nodded his head and looked away. "Sorry. I had hoped this would turn out differently, but I guess I've still got some second chakra issues to resolve."

Maggie laughed. "At our age, who doesn't?"

"It was easier in India, not the same level of temptation."

"Well, maybe you need to go back there to resolve that issue," Maggie said.

"Maybe," Thomas said tentatively. "I will miss Anna. I've grown quite attached to her."

"You know she can visit you in your dreamtime."

Thomas lowered his head. "It's not the same." He looked back and said contritely, "Sorry, Maggie. I had wanted this to turn out differently."

"I know. For me I was open either way, but it definitely swung the other way for us."

"I was planning to leave Friday. Can we take another walk on the beach? I'd liked to see Anna one more time."

"I'm sure she'd like that."

Wednesday morning was clear and sunny, and Maggie and Anna picked Thomas up at the Yoga Center, and they spent the day together walking on the beach, driving up the coast for lunch, and then stopping off and taking a walk in the woods on the drive back. Anna wanted him to stay for dinner and read to her again, but Thomas had other plans and they said their goodbyes at the Yoga Center.

Anna was sad that her father was leaving, but on the drive back to their house, she told Maggie, "He is not ready yet. But, one day. I send him love and energy; he...grow faster."

"Just don't interfere with his natural development, dear."

Anna looked at the window for a long time. "It not easy being me."

"Well, I'm glad you're you, and I wouldn't have it any other way."

Chapter 15

Anna usually lived in a state of perpetual joy, or abiding joy as the Buddhist would call it, but the sadness she felt over her father leaving was curious to her. It appeared that this talky/mental side of her became very attached to people and situations and felt badly when things didn't develop the way it wanted. In fact, it felt a fear of loss over such situations, and that was a most unpleasant emotion for her. However, experiencing these feelings and emotions did help her to understand her mother and other people better and feel real compassion for them and their plight. How had they lost the connection with their divine Self was again most curious to her. She would explore this dilemma when she was older, but for now she focused her energy on people's divine Selves and energized them. Some people naturally gravitated toward her and her energy while others shrunk away from it. She knew, as Joseph had told her, that eventually everybody would find their way back to the Divine, but she could feel their suffering and would like to alleviate it where she could.

And as she grew older her mother kept insisting that she learn to read and develop her mind. She said that if Anna was going to reach people and help them on their paths that she would need to be more familiar with the mind or the ego as Joseph called it. Anna tentatively agreed, but said she would be careful to keep it in its place, as it were, and continue to abide in her divine Self and its connection to the greater whole. But, as she learned to read and to express herself better and to use her mind to think about things, she could see the enticement and understood how in one's development most were seduced by its allure. Since the world was made of mind stuff, she assumed that you needed a large dose of it to move forward in its maze and earn its rewards, neither of which interested her.

This was one reason why she did not like to watch television or listen to the music she heard when out in the world. All of this electronic encroachment, and especially these remote talking devices everybody carried with them, defined their reality in mental terms and made it harder to see through or go beyond that realm. Since they lived in a sea of electromagnetic waves, Anna at first had trouble going to grocery stores or restaurants with her mother, because of all of this electronic vibration in the air. It wasn't until Joseph had shown her how to create a cocoon of energy around her, or strengthen her aura and use it as a filter, that she was able to move more freely in the world. She also noticed, and was somewhat amused by the fact, that some of these devices wouldn't work in her presence, or if she was annoyed by them that she merely needed to expand her aura to shut them down.

Once while sitting in the park and enjoying the sheer magnificence of nature and its subtle emanations, a teenage boy with spiked orange hair strolled in and sat down on a bench with a big boom box and began playing very loud hard rock music. It destroyed the peaceful ambience of this natural setting. Anna expanded her aura and strengthened it to the point that the boom box no longer worked. The boy kept turning the dials, but eventually he just stood up and walked off.

Her mother found this very curious. "Anna, did you do something to turn off the boy's music box?"

"Mama, it hurt my ears."

"Mine too, but I'm not sure that is the proper use of your... energies."

"It will work other places and not hurt our ears."

"Well, next time let me know and we'll just walk away."

"Yes, but it hurts the trees and the grass and the bugs in the dirt too."

Maggie didn't have an answer to this dilemma, but started to make a list of questions on which to query Joseph.

Part of the problem was her mother's fear that her state of being, as Joseph referred to it, would be discovered by others. She understood that a world ruled by mental schemes would find her consciousness threatening, and her mother was here to protect her and so she would try to be more careful with her spiritual expression. But she had to wonder if there wasn't another place on this planet that would be more accommodating. Her father had talked to her about India, and Anna wondered if they would all be happier and safer there or maybe at Ma hi' Ma's place, or the ashram as they called it.

One night while they were listening to Hindu devotional chanting or Kirtan, Anna raised the question.

"I like this music better than American. Maybe we go to India and live there instead."

As with many such questions from her spiritually precocious child, Maggie waited a moment to allow for a more heartfelt response. "I would like us to visit India someday, but if you were meant to live there, you would've been born there. Don't you think?"

Anna stared at her mother with that ageless look of hers. "But, by other mother. And I wanted you...and Daddy. We have good karma from past lives." She paused for a moment. "But now we can just move there."

"You know for decades many Indian gurus have come to live in America to help...raise the vibration of our people."

"You think I was born here for this reason?"

Maggie smiled. Her five-year-old daughter picked up on nuisances so quickly. "Yes. I was thinking that."

Anna gave this some thought. "I see. But we go visit before I get too old."

"I promise, Anna."

This seemed to settle the question, but Maggie figured it was time to visit Ma and the ashram and let Anna soak up some of its Indian vibrations. She also needed to talk with her publisher, and decided they would stop there on the way to the ashram. Jean was anxious for Maggie to write a third book since the other two had been both critical and financial successes, but she had trouble coming up with another book concept with a similar motif. The first two used Palmistry's life and heart lines, not that she was an adherent of this esoteric art, but there were no other lines that offered the same feeling tone, as Maggie would refer to it. So, for a year, she had been stifled trying to come up with another concept.

When Maggie told Anna that they would be stopping by to see Jean Millburn, her publisher, on the way to the ashram, she asked, "She want more books?"

"Yes, dear. But, we haven't been able to decide on another approach."

Anna nodded her head and thought for a moment. "Why not 'Only God'?"

Maggie didn't overreact to its overtly religious theme. "You mean how God is the life force in all things?"

Anna smiled. "Connects everybody like life lines and heart lines."

Bodhi sauntered over wanting to go out for a walk. Maggie reached over and petted him, and suddenly had the idea, "*The Dog Who was God.*"

Anna clapped her hands. "Yes, and put Bodhi picture on cover."

Maggie laughed. "I don't know about that." She stood up. "Let's go for a walk."

As they walked to the park and Anna and Bodhi played together on the grass, this book idea started to jell: how everything was a part of God or all-that-is. And using a dog as an example, given the reversal of its lettering, dog to God, gave the idea a whimsical spin, even if it would still offend some. But, given that she was trying to keep a low spiritual profile to protect her daughter from undue scrutiny, was this an invitation for some to look at them more closely? Maggie had never been a provocateur, but maybe because of Anna's influence and her own spiritual development, she wanted to use her art to explore her connection to the greater whole.

That night, after Anna went to sleep, Maggie stayed up and started to write a concept paper and sketch out some drawings. She remembered one New Age author saying that the dogs in her life were the inspirations for her bestselling books, and that a new one appeared at each stage of her own inner development. This made her wonder about Bodhi and whether his "affect" on Anna also extended to her. She had had dogs as a child and teenager and felt particularly drawn to them. Maybe this concept was inspired by Bodhi's Spirit as well.

Maggie called Jean the next morning, and she scheduled an appointment with her on Friday afternoon. The plan was to go to dinner with Jean and spend the night at her house before driving on to the ashram the next morning.

On Friday afternoon, Maggie, Anna, and Bodhi traipsed up the stairs to Millburn Publishing's second-floor offices and were escorted into Jean's office. She had set out chairs for Maggie and Anna, and seeing their golden retriever, she stepped out and found a rug in the next room and spread it out on the floor next to Anna's chair.

"Anna. You're so big now. I can't believe you're five years old."

"Oh, I much older," she stated matter-of-factly.

Jean looked to Maggie for an explanation. "We're Hindu, and she believes in reincarnation."

"I see." She smiled indulgently. "So what's this 'great new idea' that you wouldn't share over the phone?"

Maggie tentatively handed Jean her concept paper and the few sketches that she had drawn. Jean read it once, and then reread it again, and carefully looked at the drawings and sample interior illustrations. She looked up and glanced over at Bodhi.

"So, your dog is whispering in your ear instead of vice versa?" she said facetiously.

"Well, actually Anna started the ball rolling, but my applying her 'everything-is-God' concept to a dog makes it more... palatable I would imagine, but it's just an extension of the oneness theme in my first two books."

"Yes, but you're really going to get slammed by some reviewers," Jean said, and paused for a moment. "But then all of these dog books on the market are idolizing their dogs anyway and this just ups the ante. I think we can skate on the concept." Anna looked puzzled. Jean leaned over her desk in the child's direction. "We can do it without annoying too many people."

"It sad, but people not always get things," Anna said.

"Well, you've got that right, my dear." She turned to Maggie. "Okay, write me a book along this line, and let's take a look at it."

"And you'll give me an advance on this concept?" Maggie asked.

Jean smiled. "Yes, but do I make the check out to Bodhi?"

Anna clapped her hands. "He buy lots of treats."

Jean just shook her head. This child was so quick that it was amazing. She couldn't wait to develop her as an author one day.

Chapter 16

Jean agreed to take Bodhi for the weekend, and on Saturday they drove up to Ma hi' Ma's ashram, and as Maggie parked her car and followed Prema to their private quarters, she noticed several rather sickly devotees stumbling around the grounds. She found this curious and a little suspicious, but she would withhold her judgment until they met with Ma. They were escorted into the temple room where Ma was reading a book. She looked up and smiled at them and opened her arms. Anna ran to Guru and jumped into her arms. Ma closed her eyes and absorbed the energy emanating from young Anna.

"Your energy grows stronger and stronger each time I see you," Ma said, holding her on her lap.

"As this body grows, it can hold more." Anna paused for a moment. "Is that why Buddha have big belly?"

Ma shook her head. "Actually the historical Buddha was thin befitting a monk who wandered the countryside. The image of the fat Buddha is actually the Chinese monk, Hotei, whose name in Chinese is Budai, the cause of the confusion."

"I like the picture of Buddha."

"Well, Hotei was known for his kindness and generosity to children."

"You very smart, Ma."

"No, dear. But I read a lot, which your mother tells me you shy away from."

Maggie interjected, "Well, she's just starting to learn."

Anna glanced over at her mother as if to say, I can handle this. She turned back to Guru. "It easy but not direct knowing."

Ma nodded her head. "Yes, and while you, unlike most, who have to struggle to quiet the mind and receive direct knowing, never lost your divine connection, the mind will still grow in you and you must learn to deal with it."

"Beautifully said, Ma," Maggie added, realizing that there was much that could benefit Anna from her guru's instruction.

"And since we're talking about the Buddha, the opening line of *The Dhammapada*, a collection of the Buddha's teachings, says, 'All that we are is the result of what we have thought.'"

"But, if we never think thoughts, we stay what we are: divine."

Ma laughed. "Yes, child. But, just speaking as such is a kind of thinking, as pure as it is." Ma turned to Maggie. "I can see how the wise men of the temple were confounded by the child Jesus."

"I like Jesus too," Anna said, her eyes lighting up.

"Of course you do, but let me read to you from an ancient Hindu text, *The Upanishads*," Ma said, and lifting up and showing Anna the book she was reading, Ma turned to a short chapter at the end of the book. "'The Amritabindu Upanishad' says:

The mind may be said to be of two kinds,
Pure and impure. Driven by the senses
It becomes impure; but with the senses
Under control, the mind becomes pure.

It is the mind that frees us or enslaves.
Driven by the senses we become bound;
Master the senses we become free.
Those who seek freedom must master their senses.

When the mind is detached from the senses
One reaches the summit of consciousness..."

"But I already beyond senses...pure," Anna insisted.

"But, you like to walk on the beach and through the deep forest, pet Bodhi, and love to gaze into the starry night sky," Maggie added.

"These are all sense impressions, child," Ma added. "And

unless you live in a cell cut off from all of life, you will use your senses and like all of us will be tempted to become enmeshed in them."

Anna nodded her head. "So if I know more help me stay pure?"

"Yes, child. That is what your mother and I are talking about and what we wish for you."

"Very well." Anna scooted off Ma hi' Ma's lap. "All talk make me hungry. We use sense of taste now."

As they were walking to the cafeteria, Maggie broached the subject. "Coming in today I saw a few sickly people."

Ma smirked. "Yes, I confess. Megan sent us the newspaper article about the boy in San Luis Obispo who miraculously recovered from bone cancer." Maggie shook her head. "It's only the devotees, and we can keep it to ourselves." She considered this implied proposal. "The child must share her gift, be of service to others."

Maggie let out a deep sigh. She thought she had made this clear to Ma that Anna wasn't to do any wholesale healing of the sick at the ashram or elsewhere.

Anna, who had listened to their exchange, added, "Me bless food, and everybody feel better."

Ma hi' Ma's eyes lit up. "Of course. The perfect solution." She looked to Maggie who nodded her head. Ma motioned to Prema who had been following two steps behind them. "Prema, dear. Go to the kitchen and have all the bowls of food set out so Anna can bless them before we start the buffet line."

She smiled. "Not a word, Prema."

"Yes, Ma. But, not everybody shows up for lunch."

"We do dinner too," Anna interjected, settling the matter. "This make me more hungry."

Needless to say, the devotees all enjoyed their vegetarian lunch, many going back for seconds, including Ma who usually frowned upon overeating at any meal; like the Buddha she had told them, "to eat until you're not hungry, not until you are full." The effects of the super-charged lunch and dinner resulted in fewer of the devotees showing up for evening meditation. As Ma would later say, "It was their loss." Anna conducted the meditation, and the energy in the domed chamber was so palpable that Ma was almost thankful for the lower turnout, afraid that any further amplification would do structural damage to the building.

However, several devotees were too sick to attend these meals, but were still in need of a healing. The next morning, Prema gathered them and one by one they filed into the temple room for a personal healing session with Anna. All were sworn to secrecy as to the source of any recovery, which most experienced instantaneously. One lame devotee walked out of the chamber and practically did a jig in the common area, while the others healed just relaxed on benches and the lawn to acclimate to their now pain-free bodies.

Maggie watched with joy and consternation wondering how long her daughter's miraculous healing ability could be kept quiet, as she struggled with the conflict between Anna's service to others and the need to protect her sanctity from a world that shamelessly exploited the talented few. After the last of only several healings, Anna sat with her mother and Guru.

"Mama nervous about me healing people," she said.

"As am I, child," Ma added. "I did not realize the extent of your abilities, which are almost biblical. She is right to be concerned."

"Maybe we talk with Joseph?"

It was Ma hi' Ma's turn to clap her hands. Anna did the swirling upward motion with her right hand, and their spirits were once again lifted up and transported to the spring where Joseph awaited them. He was wearing the same white suit and glowed as bright as ever.

"So we're back to the same issue?" Joseph asked.

"I'm afraid so," Maggie offered.

"Don't be afraid, my dear. As I've said, the child and all who watch over her are protected. However, she has her own destiny to fulfill and healing others is part of that." He paused to let this pronouncement settle. "But walking up to strangers in the park or on the street and healing them of terminal cancer would be... counterproductive, as I believe you say these days."

"But many need help," Anna added.

"And, as I've said, many of them are working out their own karma and a gratuitous healing of them would stunt their growth opportunity."

"How does she discriminate?" Ma asked.

"Well, as I told them earlier, about the boy Martin, Anna must ask their spirits if the time is right. Even some, like those at the ashram who are devoted to you and the Hindu faith, may still not be ready and have more karma to work off."

"And even at her age Anna can recognize that?" Ma asked.

Joseph smiled. "Her spirit, which is eternal, will know, and not be pulled like the ego mind by emotional...issues."

Ma bowed her head to honor the man's wise guidance.

Joseph turned back to Anna. "That applies to sharing your wisdom as well. Many are not ready to hear...the truth of their own being." He paused. "Which is why I agree with Ma and your mother about the development of your mind, which will give you more discernment as you grow older."

Anna winced at this suggestion. "All is one, Anna," Joseph said, as he twirled his own hand and they found themselves back in the temple room.

"Wow, I wish I had him for guidance when I was struggling with my spiritual development," Ma said.

Anna smiled at her. "You helped him long time ago in Tibet. He pay back now."

Ma and Maggie just shook their heads. "Boy. I could use an ice cream fix," Maggie said to Anna's delight.

Ma added, "I believe they have some in the freezer. I'll let you get it, Maggie. Most unseemly for me to show up scrounging around for ice cream."

After Maggie left, Anna turned to Ma. "You know park and Joseph not real in our sense?"

Ma looked curiously at Anna. "And what are they?"

Anna struggled to articulate a concept. "Like movie, it shines from other...place."

Ma considered this for a moment. "A projection from another spiritual realm?"

Anna smiled. "Good guru. Mama not understand...yet."

"Yes, very advanced idea, but you work with her, be her guru."

Anna looked around and put a finger to her lips. "Our secret."

Ma laughed and nodded to her conspiratorially.

Chapter 17

Before they left on Sunday, Maggie spoke with Ma about the need to homeschool Anna, and Ma said she would take this subject up with James Edwards. A month later, a packet of information arrived with forms for Maggie to fill out. Born in late November, Anna turned five after the October 1 California deadline for kindergarten entrance the previous year, and so this school year Maggie would need to set up a private homeschool based in her apartment. She filled out the forms and sent them back to Edwards who filed them with the state. However, during this time and while these formalities were being addressed, Maggie received a surprise visit from Gary Pritchard.

After Gary was seated in the living room and served yogi tea, and Anna and Bodhi came out to join them, he took out a map of the city and spread it out on the coffee table. It had several small circles drawn on it in red.

"Maggie, I've been talking with Ma and James Edwards, and we feel that you need to move to a house with a yard to properly homeschool Anna."

"Yes, it will be a little cramped here, but I can't afford to rent a house."

Gary smiled. "I would like to buy a house and lease it to you, and set your rent at $500 a month or so, plus utilities, and I'll pay property taxes."

Maggie immediately stiffened up. Anna reached over and laid a hand on her knee. She pointed to the house near Laguna Lake. "I like that one."

"Gary, this is very kind of you, but…"

"The lease and the arrangements will be perpetual, until you decide to leave, or are able to buy it from me."

Maggie smiled. "You mean if I have a falling out with Ma, or whatever, you can't evict me?"

"Not unless you don't pay your rent," Gary added with a smirk. "Maggie, this is about Anna, not about you and Ma." He paused for a moment. "What you may not know about me is that in my twenties I lived in India with every intention of becoming a sannyasin, but my guru told me to return to America and become a householder and that someday I would be of great service to humanity. I was married and divorced and had two children, both of whom are lovely heathens. Please, let me be of service to Anna and her great unfolding."

Gary's heartfelt appeal brought tears to her eyes. Maggie looked down at the map more closely. "This location over here is closer to town and Hawthorne Elementary and to Meadow Park."

"Yes. Both locations are near public schools, the one in Laguna is blocks away from a middle school. I thought you might go back to teaching when Anna's older, and no longer needs to be homeschooled."

Anna again pointed to the house on Laguna Lake. "This one close to park too."

Gary smiled. "Well, why don't we drive over and take a look at both of them, or any of the others I've circled?"

They first stopped by the house in town on Cypress near the elementary school. It was a smaller two-bedroom house on a medium-size lot and seemed cramped for their purpose. They next drove over to the place on Oceanaire Drive across from Laguna Lake, which was much more upscale: a three-bedroom overlooking the lake with a big backyard. Gary had the key and they did a walk-through. It was perfect, but Maggie figured it would cost a fortune.

"Good investment. The price will only go up with time, and seeded with Anna's energy, who knows what I'd get for it."

Maggie turned to her daughter. "Not ocean, but water is water." She nodded her head enthusiastically.

"So it's settled?" Gary asked.

"When could we move in?" Maggie tentatively asked, still taken aback by Gary's overly generous offer.

"You've need to give a month's notice at your apartment. And I'll have to close on this property. But, by the first of the month, I think you can start moving things over. I'll hire a mover to move the big stuff."

Maggie raised her eyebrows. "I don't know what to say," she said sitting down on the back porch steps.

"Say yes, Mama," Anna said and ran out into the backyard with Bodhi.

Maggie stood up and looked at the huge living room. "You know it's large enough for me to bring in other private school students."

"Yes, there are some Hindus in the area that probably feel the same way about public schools, if not for the same reason."

Maggie wondered if this was part of his or Ma's plan, but it did seem like a natural path to follow. "Okay, Gary. I accept your offer on behalf of Anna."

"Good. And since it'll take a month to get back your deposit on the apartment, the first month's rent is free, and no deposit needed. I trust you."

Maggie started to walk through the house and make some preliminary decisions about what went where. It was much larger than her apartment, but her mother had a storage unit filled with their old furniture, in case the girls ever needed it. The deal was really closed when Gary dropped them back at her apartment: Jean Millburn's contract and advance check on *The Dog Who was God* was in the mailbox. Everything in Divine timing, she said to herself. She immediately called her mother who said she'd drive up that weekend to look over the house and create a moving plan.

When the three of them and Bodhi drove up to the Laguna Lake home, Grace was amazed. "Maggie, how can you afford this? Are you and Thomas or somebody else getting together with you?"

"No, Mother. Haven't heard from him since he went back to India." She stepped up and unlocked the door, and they walked inside. "One of Ma hi' Ma's devotees owns it, and since I'm homeschooling Anna, he felt I needed a bigger place—figure they hope I'll open a private school for other Hindus in the area."

Grace just shook her head. "Are you sleeping with the guy?"

"Mother, please. It's nothing like that. In fact, he's kinda like Anna's godfather," Maggie added, stretching the truth a bit.

"Well, as your father would say, 'never look a gift horse in the mouth.'" As they went from room to room, Grace made mental notes on what to bring up from the storage unit to fill out the space. "You could turn this third room into a guest room," Grace added, liking the north light from the window and imagining spending time here and painting.

"This is the Temple Room, but it will have a sofa bed."

Anna stepped inside as if to claim her space. Grace said to Maggie, "I didn't know you were so wedded to your religion."

"Not for mama, for me," Anna insisted. Maggie gave her a stern look that didn't escape Grace's purview.

"I see, young lady. Two rooms for you. You must be the Queen of Sheba."

"No, Daughter of Krishna."

They heard Bodhi barking from the backyard. "Anna, I believe the Bodhisattva is calling you," Grace said, shaking her head.

She smiled. "Good one, Grandma." She raced out of the room.

Grace turned to her daughter. "Okay, what aren't you telling me about Anna and this Hindu thing? I saw how the local devotees were treating her at the Chaucer Bookstore signing."

Maggie gave her mother the same stern look. "Mother, believe me, you don't want to know."

Grace was taken aback for a moment, and then she smiled. "You're probably right. It'll be too much for your heathen father. So, we'll not broach the subject, unless Anna decides to walk across the lily pond in our backyard."

Maggie smiled. "I'll warn her about doing that."

Grace just shook her head and walked out of the room. "Let's get going. I think I know what we need to bring up from Santa Barbara."

The move to the Laguna Lake home went without a hitch; Grace and Mark drove up in a rental truck filled with some old but serviceable furniture and that coincided with the arrival of Gary Pritchard's moving company van. He stepped out wearing jeans and a T-shirt and was followed by a slew of local Ma devotees, women and men, and the furniture was quickly unloaded and arranged, with curtains hung and shelves and closets filled. The Langfords liked Gary and were appreciative of his generous offer, and spending time with him allayed any suspicions of murky motives on his part. He seemed genuinely devoted to Anna. Afterward the women cooked a feast, and they had an impromptu dinner party in the backyard now filled out with the Langfords' old lawn furniture.

It took Bodhi a while to relax his guard dog duties with all of these new people milling around, but Anna communicated with him and he spent the afternoon chasing Frisbees and eating table scraps. Mark, if not Grace, was somewhat surprised by Anna being asked to say grace, but otherwise he was oblivious to the subtle homage paid to his granddaughter. The gathering was much more genteel and civilized than Mark's backyard barbecues, but he could tolerate it and was impressed with several philosophical discussions he held with two of Ma's devotees. Grace had also noticed that Maggie was a focus of a lot of young male attention herself, but her daughter seemed oblivious of it.

After everybody pitched in and cleaned up and they left the house, Grace had a glass of Chardonnay and talked with Maggie while Mark took a shower and prepared for bed. After exchanging pleasantries about her friends, Grace broached the subject that was on her mind.

"Dear, are you interested in any of these hunky young guys?"

Maggie was sipping tea and smiled at her mother's inquiry. "No, not particularly."

"Well, they're certainly interested in you. I mean, outside of your one-night fling with Thomas, I haven't heard you talk about dating anybody. Aren't you...?" Grace didn't state the obvious.

"No, mother. The yoga and my devotional practices seem to have aligned my energy along other channels."

"Well, spirituality is fine, but it's no substitute for great sex," Grace added.

"And how would you know that, Mother?" she asked, then added, "I mean, you've never been particularly spiritual."

Mark came out in his PJs. "I'm ready for bed. You girls going to fix up the sofa bed or what?"

The two women stood up and pulled out the spring bed. Maggie had set aside the linen, and they tucked in the sheets and puffed up the pillows. She sat on the edge of the bed and bounced up and down, and told her mother with a smirk, "Well, I hope the springs aren't too worn out." Grace blushed, but Mark didn't catch the reference as he pulled back the sheets on one side to slip into bed.

"Well, I'll let you get to...bed. Pleasant dreams," Maggie told them. "And thanks again for all of your help."

"Don't mention it, dear," Grace said.

Maggie went back to Anna's room, but she had fallen asleep earlier and was still sleeping soundly. She must have been worn out by all the activity. Maggie watched her daughter, amazed as always that she hardly moved an inch while sleeping, and never rolled over on her stomach or side. No doubt this was due to her spirit body's astral travels.

Later that night, Grace had a peculiar dream. Anna had come to her while she was sitting in a lawn chair and touched the base of her spine. For Grace it was like touching a live electric wire, and a stream of intense energy shot up her spine and filled her head, and as her eyes crossed and she felt ecstatic, she heard young Anna tell her, "Better than sex."

Waking up the next morning and recalling the dream, Grace laughed but could only wonder if this were her dream or Anna's implant, as she began to suspect, and if so she really didn't want to explore that possibility.

Chapter 18

In California educators can establish a private or homeschool in their homes, but they have to file an affidavit with the Superintendent of Public Instruction. James Edwards had previously filed all of the other necessary forms with the various departments, and after Maggie's affidavit was received, she was scheduled for an appointment with the private and homeschool administrator for the San Luis Coastal Unified School District.

Maggie arrived for her meeting with Mrs. Linden with a file containing all of her forms and teaching certificates. She was ushered into the woman's office. She was middle-age with wire-rimmed glasses and tight pulled-back gray hair, and had a severe look. After reviewing the paperwork, Linden looked up. "I see that you have an arts and crafts teaching degree from Berkeley, but that your elementary school teaching credits are from UC correspondence courses?"

"Yes, after I decided that I wanted to homeschool Anna, I couldn't go back to school at Berkeley or for that matter to college here, so this was more convenient." Mrs. Linden seemed less than impressed. "I did pass all the required state examinations and was rewarded a primary school teaching certificate."

Linden shuffled through the paperwork and nodded her head. She removed a document from her own folder. "Our concern is not only the education of our children but their emotional health as well. I see here that a complaint was registered and that a Ms. Beverly Foster from Child Services interviewed you about your daughter Anna several years ago."

Maggie calmed herself. "Yes, someone in the apartment complex where we lived was concerned about Anna being overly reclusive, but I addressed this issue with Ms. Foster and she seemed satisfied."

"Well, as you know from your studies, preschool is as much

about socialization as it is learning the three Rs, and establishing proper social habits for their later adult behavior, which is more difficult in a school with one child."

"That depends on the child and their needs, and I believe my own child's artistic nature requires special...attention."

"I see. You know bible class at your church on Sundays would expose Anna to children her own age."

"Well, we are Hindus, but we do attend functions if not services at the Buddhist temple in town, and she's around children at my weekly yoga class and at the park near our home."

"Well, while you're qualified to homeschool your child, I am concerned about her socialization, and I'm going to ask for psychological testing at some point in her early primary education."

"At that point, please address your concerns with my lawyer James Edwards of San Francisco, who handles legal matters for me and my Hindu guru's California devotees. I'll leave his address and phone number."

"Why so?"

"Anna, even at her age, meditates and has an intense inner life, which is why she is 'reclusive,' I believe the earlier complaint read."

Ms. Linden frowned but was sufficiently chastised. "I see. Well, that won't be necessary." She gathered up Maggie's material and placed it back in her file, stood up and handed it back to her. "Thank you for coming in and I wish the best for you and Anna."

As Maggie turned to leave, Ms. Linden added, "Have my secretary copy your certificates for our files."

After Maggie left, Mrs. Linden made a note in her file that while Margret Langford was qualified to homeschool her child, there was something unusual about her and her child's religious situation and she required further monitoring at some future date. She also noted that her Oceanaire Drive home was only blocks from Laguna Middle School, and so she would tell the head of the PTA there to ask around about Mrs. Langford and her Anna.

In September at the start of the school year, Maggie set up a schedule for Anna's instruction on a daily basis. She had studied and was impressed with the German school educator Freidrich Froebel who established the first kindergarten in 1837. He used symbols as his primary teaching aide, and especially encouraged arts and craft activities. For him the garden symbolized the importance of play in a child's early education. Maggie also spent several days at the local Montessori School asking questions of their kindergarten teachers, having read Maria Montessori's ideas on educating children years ago. So while Anna preferred drawing and painting, they now also used Legos to build things and construction paper for cutouts as well, and played with voice toys that spoke the letters of the alphabet, or Anna's favorite: the names of animals. So, every morning or afternoon, given their mutual schedule, time was devoted to such school activities, and if weather permitted at least twice a week they walked down to the park after normal school hours so she could play with other children.

Maggie also began teaching her to read, if only at a preliminary level. After the recent talks with Ma and Joseph, Anna understood the importance of developing her mind and learning the skills needed to communicate with others. However, she also insisted that an equal amount of time be devoted to meditation, and maybe because of that discipline Anna seemed to be very single-focused, a form of active meditation, with everything she did. There was, at least at this point, no inner chatter or, as some called it, "monkey mind." She was clear and centered and even-tempered almost all the time. Maggie wondered if she and Anna might collaborate on a book someday about maintaining this balance between the inner and outer worlds. This would be especially directed to children developing but not becoming obsessed with the mind, always being centered and using the mind as a tool and not over identifying with it and its obsessions.

For Anna including more outer activities only increased the depth of her inner focus and journeying, like a tether that grounded her. Unlike most people's meditations, which was mainly to quiet the mind and connect it to their divine source or soul, Anna actively engaged in a kind of inner development. With Joseph as her guide, they would travel to other realms and she would receive, if not instruction — which was a mental concept — an infusion of spiritual energy with its own special evolutionary powers. In these realms beings were conscious creators of their worlds or dimensions, and the 3D physical realm in which Anna found herself was greatly affected by their activities. It became clear to Anna that as she grew older her mission would not be to instruct people as much as being a conduit for this energy into her world. This was what she had sensed and accounted for some of her resistance to standard education, and at some time in the future she would explain this to her mother. However, she would need to devote more time to the woman's spiritual development before she could properly understand this concept.

Anna's energy not only greatly affected Maggie but Bodhi as well. Joseph had told her that this would be Bodhi's last lifetime as a dog, and that due to his exposure to Anna's energy, he would next incarnate as a human. He had explained to her how all of life was evolving from lower or less complex forms — in regard to how much spiritual energy they could contain — to higher forms. As an example he himself had been a human being for many lifetimes before he was able to evolve into a strictly spiritual being, and that this may also be Anna's last lifetime as a human, and that part of his guidance and "instruction" was to facilitate that transition.

Anna was greatly relieved to hear of this possibility. While she was still young and even though she could recall many of her own past lives, she found this body and its expression too limited. Interacting with the celestial beings of these other realms only made that clearer to her. However, Joseph insisted that she focus on her current state of being and its development and contribution to humanity's elevation before she thought of moving on. He told her that this was the downfall of some in her position, who had foreshortened their own lives to leap forward as they imagined it, only to find themselves back again in the human realm and at a lower rung on the spiritual ladder, as it were. Anna was sufficiently admonished.

Chapter 19

That fall, only a month after Maggie had started the kindergarten homeschooling of Anna, she was sitting on a bench in the park and watching her daughter and Bodhi playing. There was a chill in the air and Anna had worn her red parka, one she had picked out to match the reddish color of her dog's coat. She loved to point out, "Look mom, we twins," to which Bodhi always barked. A short dark-skinned man, evidently Indian, with his young son approached her.

"Miss Langford," he said and bowed slightly.

"Yes."

"I'm Agam Chandra, and this is my son, Gish." Maggie nodded and let him proceed. "I've been told that you are homeschooling your daughter, Anna, and that the two of you are of the Hindu faith."

"Yes, that's correct. How can I help you?"

"Do you mind if we sit down?" Maggie nodded her head and scooted to the end of the bench to give them room. "I'm also told that you are devotees of Sri Ma hi' Ma, and are particularly devout."

Maggie smiled. "Well, Mr. Chandra, I don't know who you've been talking to, but I doubt that Ma would characterize me as such."

Chandra smiled. "Modesty in a Western woman is commendable." He paused for a moment. "I am wondering if you would be so kind to take on my son as a kindergarten student. He is very bright and will be an excellent scholar one day, and I wish that he get special attention in a devout setting."

Maggie had considered taking on other students but thought she'd wait until the first grade at least. She looked around him and smiled at Gish, properly dressed in his short pants and blue blazer. The boy smiled back and seemed to be sweet and mild-mannered. Maggie closed her eyes and felt an up charge of energy that usually indicated a positive situation. She opened her eyes and waved Anna over.

"Anna, this is Gish. Why don't the two of you play with Bodhi while I talk with his father?"

Anna smiled, put out her hand, which Gish took and they walked over to the swing set, where she sat him in the swing and began pushing him.

"Your daughter is rather forthright," Chandra said, slightly taken aback.

"She's no wilting flower, that's for sure." Maggie turned to Agam. "So, why don't you tell me a little about yourself and your family and your expectations for your son?"

Chandra had to smile, like mother like daughter, he thought to himself. He told Maggie that he and his wife, Jade, were from New Delphi. His father was a university professor, and he met his wife at the university and they were married after they both graduated. He majored in business, and after graduation he started to work for an international trading company, and several years later he was sent to San Francisco to open a warehouse and manufacturing outlet. He and his wife didn't like Western city life, and on a vacation had traveled through San Luis Obispo and loved it here. So they moved and he opened his own business. They have two children, Gish and his younger sister Rai.

Maggie waved Anna and Gish over. "Anna, would you like Gish to be homeschooled with you at our house?"

Anna gave this careful consideration. "He is a very nice boy; I hope he likes to meditate."

Maggie looked to his father. "Well, both his mother and I meditate, but thought he was too young to learn, but if Anna would be so kind as to instruct him, I'm sure he'll like that." Agam turned to his son, who eagerly nodded his head. Maggie motioned for them to resume their play.

"I must say, Miss Langford. Your daughter is quite

extraordinary."

"Mr. Chandra. If I share something with you, can you keep it to yourself?" Agam nodded his head. "I think you need to know what your son will be exposed to." She paused, as Chandra raised his eyebrows. "My daughter was born totally awakened, and has a spiritual vibration that can be quite overwhelming to others."

Agam stared at Maggie for a long moment to gauge the sincerity of this statement. "Ms. Langford, my family has a long history of religious devotion, and it has been blessed with several religious adepts down through the ages. I can't think of a more auspicious situation for my son." He laughed wholeheartedly. "You must meet my wife, Jade. She'll be dropping Gish off for lessons, and she'll just love Anna and you. So, let's make our arrangements."

The following Monday Jade Chandra dropped her son Gish off at Maggie's house. The woman was wearing a blue Western skirt and a white blouse with a colorful red scarf. Maggie showed them both inside, and the boy immediately ran over to where Anna was building a ship with Legos. After the customary introductions, Maggie walked Jade over to the alcove overlooking the backyard and poured cups of yogi tea for them. For a moment they watched Bodhi running around the yard chasing a sparrow. Finally Jade broached the subject that was of most interest to her. "My husband tells me that Anna was born self-aware?"

"Yes, and as I told…Agam, if you don't mind me referring to him by his first name?"

Jade smiled. "No. Not at all."

"It is not something I share with others, but given the circumstances…"

Jade reached out and laid her hand on Maggie's. "I understand, and you have our utmost discretion."

Maggie could feel a tingle of energy from the touch of her

hand, which reassured her. "Anna began talking to me before she was born, insisted that I buy only vegan food at the store."

Jade laughed. "Oh, how delightful. And after she was born?"

"She would come to me in my dreams or talk with me telepathically during the day about matters that concerned her."

"And today?"

"She has a spirit guide, Joseph, who whisks her off to other spiritual realms for instruction."

Jade eyes narrowed. "A Westerner?"

"Well, he appears as such."

"I would've thought, being of the Hindu faith, that he would be Indian."

Maggie smiled. "I don't think appearance is big priority over there."

Jade nodded her head and smiled sheepishly. "Yes, of course. Hate to sound ethnocentric."

Anna and Gish stepped over to the table and looked around for the customary plate of cookies. "Anna, this is Gish's mother, Jade."

The girl turned to her with a gaze was so full of love and sanctity that Jade put her hands together and bowed. Anna stepped over and touched her arm. The surge of energy almost overpowered the woman. She started to cry. Maggie stood up and retrieved some tissues from a box on the nearby counter.

Anna closed her eyes, and then opened them. "Joseph says your grandmother Isa teaches in one of their schools."

Filled with emotion, Jade stood up and ran to the nearby bathroom. Maggie turned to her daughter. "Anna, why don't you and Gish go outside and play with Bodhi before we start class."

"Not mean to upset her, Mommy."

"We'll talk about it later. Go now."

Maggie refilled their teacups and set out some of rice crackers and black bean hummus. After a while Jade returned, her eyes still red; she sat down and took a sip of tea and dipped a cracker in the hummus and munched on it.

"Sorry. But my grandmother was so precious to me, and hearing about her kind of overwhelmed me."

"I understand, and Anna needs to learn to be more discrete."

Jade vigorously shook her head. "Oh no, no, no. Don't admonish her for being who she is."

"But, as you can imagine, that has been a topic of discussion between Joseph, me, and Ma hi' Ma."

Jade nodded her head. "Yes, I would imagine in this culture that such an expression would be alarming to some and can see why you chose homeschooling." She stood and picked up her purse. "My husband and I are so happy to have met you and Anna and for you accepting Gish into your school. It will be a... great education for him, as if he were in an ashram."

Maggie walked her to the door. "On sunny days, we usually walk to the park along the lake after lessons, and you can pick Gish up there today, if you like, after three o'clock."

They shook hands with good eye contact and Jade left.

As Maggie walked across the living room to the backyard to gather her students, she thanked Lord Krishna for bringing such a wonderful family into their lives and looked forward to the lessons they would bring. During the first few weeks of schooling, it became evident that Gish was mentally precocious and that he was very good at arithmetic, or so it seemed to Maggie from their preliminary explorations of the subject. This seemed to spark Anna's interest in her studies. At first Maggie wondered if her renewed interest was competitive, but figured that was her own projection. Anna liked Gish and seemed interested in what interested him. However, the boy seemed less inclined to meditate and in other spiritual pursuits, which was curious to Anna and provided a lesson of its own.

One night after dinner and their nightly walk with Bodhi, Anna asked, "Mama, why does Gish not like to meditate? He is smart."

Maggie closed her eyes and gathered her inspiration. "Anna, in most of us, the development of the mind and ego comes first, even in those given a spiritual or religious education."

Anna thought about this for a moment. "But, as children, if spiritual devotion came first, would it not make difference?"

"Even a spiritual education is partly a mental experience."

"But, if children meditate and are one with the divine, like me, would they not be more whole?"

"I suppose they would be, but we have to honor Gish's own inclination." Anna nodded her head but was still bothered by the topic. "But, there is a reason why Gish found his way here, and I'm sure that by just following your own…inclinations, he will get what he is meant to learn from you."

Anna nodded her head. "Mama, you smart sometimes too."

"See. You're rubbing off on me."

Anna looked at her with those all-knowing Buddha eyes. "I wish we rub off some of the dark spots in your aura."

Maggie smiled, accustomed to her daughter's precocious spiritual insights. She took her head. "In time, my dear, in time."

This did bring up a concern of hers. Being exposed to her daughter's elevated energy 24/7 had greatly advanced her own spiritual development, but that was mostly by osmosis, which is what happened to Ma's devotees at the ashram. However, this was no substitute for her own spiritual practice, and she needed to apply herself more assiduously. She was not inclined to meditate for long periods of time like Anna, but realized that on their walks in the park and on the beach, there was more of an opportunity to focus on the natural world to quiet her monkey mind or concerns. Maggie had noticed, especially on walks along the seashore, that Anna rarely spoke and seemed to become one with her surroundings, which was a kind of active meditation. She decided to include more excursions into nature or even mountain treks into their outings, and use it to expand

and quiet her mind further and hopefully nurture her own spiritual aliveness.

Chapter 20

Over the school year as Maggie instructed Anna and Gish, and as they had constant daily interactions, she began to notice a change in her daughter. She was becoming more balanced between her inner and outer lives, and more socially oriented than Maggie would have expected given her earlier reluctance. Likewise Gish was developing an inner life and was meditating with Anna instead of taking afternoon naps. What also helped was that Agam and Jade invited them to celebrate Hindu and secular holidays at their home with its large garden and palatial setting and with plenty of friends who had children Anna's age. Jade and Maggie had become close, and Maggie felt more comfortable with her and Agam than with many of her Western friends, even Ma hi' Ma's devotees. She wondered about this difference and attributed it to them having grown up in the sacred Indian culture, or the last remnants of it as the new generation became more and more Western, especially given their high-tech orientation. But, Maggie also became aware that these celebrations were attended by several local unattached Indian men who went out of their way to interact with Maggie and her daughter. After turning down social invitations from several of the men, Maggie decided it was time to have a talk with Jade.

"You don't want to find a husband for yourself and a father for Anna?" Jade asked innocently to her friend's entreaty.

Maggie smiled as they sat in the alcove of her house having tea one morning, and watched Anna and Gish playing in the backyard with Bodhi. "No, or at least I don't feel inclined that way." Jade stared at her with mild concern. "I know, it doesn't seem…natural, but Anna has opened up a whole new dimension of spirituality to me, and it seems sufficient right now."

"You know all of these men are meditators and come

from devout families, or I wouldn't have invited them to our celebrations."

"They are all lovely men and a good catch, as we say, for most women, but not me, or not now."

Jade nodded her head. "I've heard you talk about Anna's father, Thomas. Is there some possibility there?"

"I had wondered about that, and had even invited him down last year, but neither of us seemed inclined to pursue a relationship, or maybe weren't...ready is a better word."

Jade reached out and touched Maggie's hand. "I understand. I'll pass the word to all these brokenhearted would-be suitors." Jade smiled. "And I won't invite them to our gatherings in the future."

Maggie immediately shook her head. "Oh, no. Don't do that. They seem like your extended family. And I really enjoy their company, if not their romantic attention."

That afternoon, after Jade had picked up Gish at the park, and while Maggie and Anna walked Bodhi around the lake, her daughter asked, "Mrs. Chandra not happy about something?"

"You noticed?"

"Her aura is usually rose colored, but dark today."

Maggie laughed. There was no hiding anything from this child. "I just told her I was not interested in her male friends in a romantic way."

Anna smiled. "You are waiting for Daddy?"

"No, dear. I'm just content the way I am, or the way we are."

Anna nodded her head and was quiet for a while. Finally she spoke up. "Maybe it is time we spoke to Joseph."

"Anna, Joseph is your spirit guide, not mine."

Anna gave her mother one of those ageless looks. "Joseph feeds the God in both of us." With that she walked ahead with Bodhi and allowed her mother time to absorb this wisdom.

Over the next few days Maggie could see Anna looking for opportunities to shift them to Joseph's garden, but she was disinclined to follow through on her daughter's invitation, which the girl honored. She had often found herself in the same position with her guru Ma hi' Ma when dealing with spiritual challenges, and would seek out her own answers first before asking Ma her perspective. She felt gurus were Wayshowers and not substitute parents for the spiritually immature, and preferred to take the lead in her own development. While the coupling that had produced Anna was mostly the result of a physical attraction, she now felt that it was also driven by some higher aspect of herself that seemed to have made the choice for her. Given the result she was inclined to seek its guidance. So Maggie posed the question, "why am I choosing a celibate life," and waited for synchronistic revelation.

Days later she received a flyer in the mail from the Bodhi Path Center, announcing a guest lecture by one of the leaders of the worldwide Kundalini Yoga movement. While Maggie mostly practiced Hatha yoga, she had had kundalini awakening experiences, or so they had seemed to her, and figured a lecture about raising energy up the spine to the higher centers may be an answer to her earlier request. So two weeks later she took Anna with her to the lecture on a balmy Friday night. Standing in line she noticed several women looking askance at her, and figured it was about bringing a child to such a heady lecture. When questioned about this issue on other such occasions, she had simply told people that "Anna reads the energy behind words she may not understand and discerns their meaning," and left it at that.

Swami Ananda, an elderly man with long locks of gray hair, a high creased forehead, and kind brown eyes, did not speak about the techniques of yoga that could raise one's energy to the ultimate crown chakra opening, but about the importance of moral principles and a sacred lifestyle. He told of how too many Westerners use intense yoga practices or tantric sex to speed up the process of awakening the kundalini, like everything else they do, but in their lives they fill their minds with depictions of graphic sex and violence and their bodies with tainted food. "The soil must be fertile for the divine seed to be nourished and to spring to life." Looking around Maggie saw that many in the audience were looking for quick fixes, and this formula did not sit well with them. Afterward most made their way out of the hall. Maggie took Anna up to Swami who was talking with a few of the more receptive attendees in front of the stage.

Swami was listening to one of them when his eyes found Anna and followed her down the aisle. Noticing the shift in his attention, the woman stopped talking and stepped back. Swami knelt down and Anna ran into his arms. After a long embrace, Swami lifted her up and sat her on the edge of stage. He turned to Maggie and just stared at her for a while.

"You know?"

"I do, Swami."

The others leaned forward trying to make sense of this cryptic exchange. Swami looked deeply at Maggie and then took her aside. "I know of what you seek. The passage way is opened, just allow the child to touch the bottom of your spine."

Maggie bowed her head. Swami stepped back to Anna. "So child, what make you of what I said?" This raised a few eyebrows among his small adult audience.

Anna sagely nodded her head. "All things are awakened by the grace of God."

Swami smiled. He turned to Maggie. "You must bring the child to India...when the time is right."

"My daddy lives in India," Anna added.

Swami looked at Anna closely. "Ah, so it is Thomas, Vinanda's Kundalini Yoga teacher," Swami said, nodding his head. "I shall have a word with Swami V."

Maggie was not sure of what the holy man planned, but she had long ago released her own designs on Thomas and his part in their lives. The lights in the hall blinked, and the group walked up the aisle and strolled out into the warm night. Swami's female assistant gave Maggie a card with his contact information, and then whisked him away to the airport for his trip to San Francisco and the next stop on his U.S. tour.

Driving back from the event, Maggie looked over at Anna who was uncharacteristically quiet. "Soon, Mommy, we go to India to visit Daddy."

"So you've got it all planned for us?" Maggie asked factiously.

"No, Mommy. I just read God's plan better."

Maggie laughed. What could she say to that retort?

When they arrived home, Anna asked. "You ready?"

Maggie looked at her daughter. She could not have heard what Swami had said to her privately. "Ready for bed?"

Anna shook her head impatiently. "Ready to poke the snake."

Maggie just shook her head in amazement. This was a common phrase about awakening the body's kundalini energy that was often characterized as a snake winding its way up the spinal cord. "Let's wait, Anna. Mommy is tired tonight."

Anna nodded her head and placed her small hand on her mother's arm in a precociously reassuring manner. They stepped out of the car and walked into the house, and they both quickly prepared for bed. Maggie dreamed that night of Thomas and making love with him, and woke up hot and bothered, and wondering how long she could wait to "poke the snake," but of course, this was not what Swami had indicated or had even warned against: sexual congress in and of itself. There may be another step, and she waited for that to appear in her life.

Chapter 21

After that night Maggie had several more dreams of making love to Thomas and then of other men she knew. At some point she either had to follow through on this inclination and date, or begin the awakening process that Swami had suggested. So, a little at lost on how to proceed and not wanting to rush into it, she agreed to talk with Joseph. Anna again magically transported their spirits to his celestial garden where he was sitting dressed in his customary white suit on a marble bench at the lily pond. They took a seat on the bench across from him. He closed his eyes in meditation and they did the same. Time passed and at some point Maggie was prompted to open her eyes and found Joseph smiling at her.

"From what I gather, sacred sex is no longer as sacred as the ancient tantric tradition had once intended it," Joseph said.

"Yes, it seems, from what I've heard, to be more about slow sex than anything sacred, or an excuse for promiscuity."

Maggie was just a bit uncomfortable talking about this subject with her daughter present and glanced at her.

Joseph smiled. "Anna is in her spirit body and ageless at this moment. Not a child, despite her appearance." Maggie nodded her head. "The premature or precipitous awakening of the kundalini energy can be harmful to the unprepared."

"As I've heard and why I'm here."

Joseph stared at her and Maggie could almost feel the tendrils of energy reaching out to her. "I believe, however, that this awakening of energy would be more advantageous than the customary alternative, which seems to have brought you here." Maggie smiled. "But, what I would advise, unlike this swami's suggestion, is that you focus on clearing your chakras one by one first...to open the way."

"And Anna would know how to do that?" Maggie asked

tentatively.

"She can add energy that will flush out what one of your more advanced swamis calls 'incompletions' or the ego's disconnected thoughts, desires, and fixations that sap your energy."

"Sounds like a long-term project."

"If it were quick and easy, everybody would sign up," Joseph said.

Maggie nodded her head, and then there was a shift of energy and they were back on the sofa in their living room.

"So, you ready, Mama?" Anna asked.

"As I'll ever be."

Anna closed her eyes as if getting instructions and told her mother to turn over on the sofa and lie on her stomach. Maggie did that and Anna laid her hand at the bottom of her mother's spinal column around the coccyx, or tailbone. The energy emanating from Anna's hand created a swirling pattern somewhat like a vortex, if one could see it, that penetrated and flushed out the karmic residue in her first or root chakra. After a while Anna removed her hand to allow the energy to settle into this chakra.

Maggie could feel the warmth surrounding her lower spine which stirred up feelings about support and safety, or the lack thereof during periods of her life. This was the root chakra's focus. She instinctively knew to just "feel" the feelings as they arose, and eventually the energy dissipated or seemed to be absorbed by the body, and new feelings arose in their place. She rolled over on her back; Anna had turned the lights down and retired to her bedroom. Maggie just lay there as new feelings arose, these about family and support issues, her father's expectations for her, his disappointment that she didn't become an academic like him. Other episodes in her childhood arose when she didn't agree with or follow through on suggestions by the adults around her, including priests and teachers, who would subtly withdraw their support. This went on for several hours, and as she felt her way through each level of the first chakra, and there seemed to be seven of them, the energy became integrated.

Finally Maggie stood up and prepared herself for bed, knowing that this was just the start of a long process. She first stepped into his daughter's room and kissed her on the forehead. "Thank you, Angel." In the dim light it seemed like Anna smiled in her sleep.

Maggie allowed this clearing to settle in for a month or so, and when she felt that her first chakra was sufficiently "tuned up," Anna repeated this clearing with her mother's second or sex chakra. After twenty minutes or so, Anna withdrew her energy and told Maggie that she would have to perform this clearing in stages, but she could begin to integrate what this first session had brought up. Maggie understood and thanked her daughter, who again retired to her bedroom and quickly fell asleep. From the first touch of her hand and the circulation of energy in this chakra, images arose that were rather distasteful for her. The "prettification of children" in our culture, especially young girls, has often made them the unconscious focus of repressed or blatant sexual energies in their parents and other adults. Maggie recalled as a six-year-old being made-up with lipstick and mascara in a party dress cut so short to reveal her panties at every turn. "Oh, how precious she looks," were calls from the adult birthday party guests, many of whom would bounce her on their knees or hold her on their laps. It was all rather unconscious and nothing overt, but it was a premature exposure and she now was able to clear this residue of her unconscious resentment of these incidents. This was followed by the sexual games children play, and then onto her teenage years where the games weren't so innocent. It took nearly three hours to integrate only some of this sexual clutter, but it was a good start.

Maggie needed nearly three sessions and two months to clear and process her second chakra, but the other chakra clearings, especially the higher ones, were much easier since they had less emotional clutter. After the final clearing of the crown chakra, Maggie felt ready to initiate, if not a sexual relationship, an intimate coupling to arouse her kundalini energy. She was constantly dreaming of making love to Thomas, and kept looking at the men she came in contact with in a more carnal light. Maggie was beside herself. She couldn't discuss this subject with her daughter, because as spiritually precocious as she was, Anna was still a child and her mother deemed such talk inappropriate. Finally, after a partially vigorous yoga workout at the Center, Maggie approached one of her fellow students, a twentysomething graphic designer named Paul Whistler. He had once asked her out, and she had demurred, but now she pulled Paul aside and asked if that date offer was still a possibility.

"You bet. Want to take in a movie, or dinner and a movie?"

"Dinner sounds wonderful."

"Great. How about I pick you up and we're go to the Granada Bistro."

"Oh, in the historic district. I've heard it's quite nice." Paul eagerly nodded his head. "But, why don't I meet you there, and I can follow you home afterward."

Paul was taken aback. "Oh, okay. Sounds like a plan. How about Friday, seven o'clock?"

Maggie agreed, gave the rather overwhelmed man a big hug, and went back to the group to pick up her daughter.

On the drive home, Anna said that her mother had a really big red aura tonight. Maggie didn't pursue the comment any further. She called Megan, the midwife who had accompanied them on the first national book tour, and she was thrilled to babysit Anna on Friday and spend the night if needed.

When Maggie broke the news of her date to Anna and that Megan would be coming over to babysit, her daughter paused for a moment and then said, "Joseph says to breathe deeply and focus on your heart chakra."

Maggie broke out laughing. Getting tantric sex advice from a spirit guide conduced through her six-year-old daughter was quite bizarre, but their whole situation was also rather wacky to say the least.

"I'll take that under consideration, dear."

Dinner was a marvelous affair. While Paul, who wasn't a vegetarian, ate fish, Maggie had the chef put together a steamed vegetable plate with a Mediterranean flair. They both had a glass of wine, the first for Maggie in quite some time, but she felt she would need to be a little high to close this deal, as it were.

After the waiter cleared their plates and neither wanted desert, it was time to test the waters. "Paul, I know this is rather forward of me, but it's been a while and we do get on fairly well, so I was wondering..."

Paul smiled but there was nothing lascivious about it. "I've bought some candles, and I'm all yours."

"Well, I'm hoping that you've had some...tantric experience, because I am interested in more than sex."

"I would hope so." He paused, a twinkle in his eye. He paid the bill, and the two of them left. Paul had an apartment on California Boulevard, with an extra parking space for guests—helpful since the street parking was mostly taken. His apartment was furnished with a Spanish or New Mexican flair, with its ornate red and royal blue sofa and chair upholstery designs. There were also several Native America pictures on the wall. Paul offered to make tea, but Maggie said, "Show me the bedroom."

Their sexual coupling was easy and fluid as if they were practiced partners. Maggie insisted that she straddle Paul so she could better control the rhythm of their conjoining. She moved slowly and then quickly, but as soon as he became too excited, Maggie slowed her pace. Focusing on her heart chakra, she began to feel the kundalini energy start to reverse it channel and move up her spine. Maggie closed her eyes as a sudden burst of energy rose up to her head and filled it with sparkling white light, as she began to twitch and shutter under the impact of this awakened energy. This lasted for ten minutes while Paul watched her counter-orgasmic high in amazement. Finally, Maggie rolled off of him, and still flushed with the energy she told him to fulfill himself. He did and rather quickly, and they laid there wrapped in each other's arms, Maggie's eyes still twitching under the impact of the "kundalini flush," as she had heard it called.

Hours later, with Paul still asleep, Maggie rolled out of bed, dressed, left a note for him, and drove home. Megan and Anna were sound asleep in her bed, and so Maggie pulled a blanket out of the closet and slept on the sofa, but as soon as she was relaxed and her eyes were closed, the energy just pulsed through her for the remainder of the night.

Chapter 22

In the fall Maggie accepted two more students into her school, both of Indian descent, but their families had immigrated to the United States years earlier, and they were more Americanized than Gish, or Anna for that matter. Devi, who called herself Debby, was half-Indian with lighter skin but dark eyes and hair. Amir was darker and went by his given name, since as he told everybody, it meant rich and prosperous in Hindi. This was the first grade, and Maggie had prepared for more formal instruction by acquiring the appropriate books and a first-grade syllabus from a teacher at Hawthorne Elementary in town. The two new students, like Anna and Gish, had attended kindergarten and had some elementary reading skills, and they would work on improving their reading and comprehension. The syllabus identified one of the key components of this first year's instruction: being able to discern the main idea of a story or picture and to differentiate between fact and fantasy. The first would be easy for Maggie to communicate and test, but given Anna's spiritual orientation, the second might be harder, at least for her, to tell apart.

However, the first challenge Maggie encountered was not instructional. When it was time for their afternoon naps that first day, Anna and Gish sat on their mats and meditated, while Debby and Amir looked on.

"What are they doing?" Amir asked.

"Meditating."

"What's that," Debby asked.

"It's like resting but not sleeping or thinking of anything."

"That's stupid," Amir said and lay down on his mat.

Debby wasn't so sure. "Can you show me?"

Maggie smiled at her. "Yes, but not today. Just lay down and take a nap, and we'll slowly show you how do that, if you still want to."

As the weeks progressed, instruction did not prove to be a problem for any of the children. They were all very bright and quickly understood and could recall the main and supporting facts and details of what they read, or as was more often the case, a story Maggie read to them. Eventually Debby, who was captivated by Anna's quiet energy, asked for instruction and began to meditate with her and Gish, much to Amir's displeasure. Then one day Amir awoke to find Anna swaying during her meditation moved by the energy flowing through her.

Amir at least waited until she opened her eyes to question her. "Why were you doing that?"

Maggie started to answer for her daughter, but Anna gave her mother one of her I'll-take-care-of-it looks and turned to Amir. "When you quiet the mind, you become one with all the energy around you, and it moves me sometimes."

Amir considered this explanation for a moment. "So you get filled up with it, and can use it like Superman?"

"Or, it can use you like Mighty Mouse," Anna replied.

Amir just nodded his head; he wasn't ready to do this strange practice, but he knew that energy was equated with power, and he definitely wanted more of that. This was not a concept that Debby would have entertained; she just felt better being around Anna and whatever the social arrangement, she sat next to her soaking up the amazing energy.

Winter came and the temperature dropped to the 40s during the day, but none of the children developed colds or came down with the flu bug when it got passed around the community, including Maggie. The children nor their parents thought anything of it. But, one day Amir was in the backyard during recess and fell off the monkey bars and hit the ground hard, and he couldn't move his arm when he was helped up. Maggie was afraid that he had broken it and was about to take him to the nearby medical clinic. Anna stepped over and touched his arm. Amir pulled away but Anna persisted, and pretty soon his arm was feeling better and they went on playing together. However, upon hearing this story, Amir's mother took him to their doctor the next day. He x-rayed the arm and could detect a slight fracture of the bone, but it seemed to have quickly mended itself. He could not explain how.

When asked by his doctor about the incident, Amir merely said that Anna touched it and it felt better and he could move it normally after that. His mother thought nothing of it, but the doctor became curious and made a note to himself. But, almost instinctively, the children turned to Anna when any of them scratched a knee, or didn't feel well. Maggie started to notice this supplication, and she again became alarmed that Anna's natural healing abilities would become known to the greater world.

One night she asked her daughter if healing every scratch and bruise of her classmates was advantageous.

"It is God that heals them, not me. You want me to say no to God?"

Maggie laughed to herself. How could she answer such a reply? "Well, next time just ask God first, or their spirit, as Joseph has instructed you. Maybe God has another plan for them."

Anna nodded her head. "Yes, Mama."

Several weeks later, when Anna was sitting next to her on the sofa one night, while Maggie read to her from the Hindu *Upanishads*, Anna said, "Debby stubbed her toe today, and I asked, and it felt like it was better for her to deal with it."

Soon Amir was meditating with the other children during their nap break, and began to lose some of his hard edge and aggressive tendencies. His father noted that, and asked Amir about his instruction at school. He told him about reading and writing and reciting poetry, and meditating. His father took exception with that, and asked for a parent/teacher meeting with Maggie in December. Hari and Parmita came in the early evening, having left Amir home with a babysitter, and they sat in the living room and sipped tea.

Finally Hari got to the point of their meeting. "Ms. Langford, we are pleased with Amir's instruction. I've had him read for me and write out something, and I was surprised by his facility at this young age."

"Your son is very smart, Mr. Kumar, and picks things up readily."

He nodded. "We understand that this isn't a private school but a homeschool situation. We wanted the smaller class setting with only a few students, but I was not aware that this included religious instruction."

"Well, nothing actually yet, but all the students are Hindu, and my daughter and I are devotees of the guru Ma hi' Ma, and so eventually religious instruction will be included."

"Eventually?" Kumar asked. Maggie nodded. "But my son is meditating."

"My daughter has been meditating since she was three years old. She comes by it naturally, and meditates instead of taking a nap, and the other students have chosen to follow her lead."

"Your daughter...from age three. I find that rather...unusual."

"Would you like to meet her?"

Hari looked to his wife who nodded her head. "Yes. That would be welcomed."

Maggie stood and went back to Anna's bedroom and told her that Amir's parents would like to meet her. Anna along with Bodhi followed Maggie back to the living room. Anna took a seat next to her mother, and Bodhi sat on the floor in front of her.

"Anna, you have a lovely golden retriever. What is his name?" Hari asked.

"Bodhi, after Bodhisattva," she said. "My mother writing book called *The Dog Who was God*."

Hari looked surprised and turned to Maggie. "It's a children's book," she added hurriedly.

"So, you think your dog is God?" Hari asked Anna with a

smirk.

"Everybody and everything part of God. Why not my dog?"

Hari was rather taken aback by Anna's forthright response. "Your mother tells me that you've been meditating since you were three."

"Before that, while I was lying in my crib, but I couldn't cross my legs."

Hari and Parmita just stared at the child. Finally, Parmita bowed her head. "I think you are a bodhisattva yourself, dear child."

Anna put a finger to her lips. "Don't tell anybody. It's our secret."

Hari shook his head in amazement. He turned to Maggie. "I am not a religious person per se, but I am moved by your daughter's presence and am confident that her influence will be helpful to my son's development."

Anna smiled. "Your mother Durga thinks so too."

Hari looked back at Anna in astonishment, tears rolling down his face at the mention of his dead mother. He finally choked out, "Well, give her my love."

Maggie just shook her head. How could she contain such a child?

Chapter 23

This first year of formal instruction for Anna and the other children progressed rather evenly. The girls were more fluent in reading and writing, and the boys in arithmetic—just adding and subtracting at this point. Maggie was still in touch with her teacher friends from the elementary school in town, and they told her this was to be expected. She realized that she had secretly hoped that Anna's presence would create a more whole-brain integration in the other students exposed to her elevated energy. Maggie came to realize that this was her expectation, and that she needed to allow Anna's effect on them to take its own course, as it had with her. But the schooling had slowed down work on her next children's book and led to repeated inquiries from Jean Millburn after Maggie missed her submission date. So over the last three months of the school year, she finished the book and finally sent it off to her publisher who was impressed with its blend of metaphysical thought and "dog magic." She scheduled its publication for late November. It would again require another publicity jaunt, which Maggie could only fit in during the school's Christmas break. This was workable for the publisher, and she would make adjustments to the schedule.

This writing again reinforced in her mind the instructional value of the story art form, which had been used through the ages to convey higher spiritual meaning. While she had not planned to include religious instruction in the first year, she was moved to read her class a children's version of *The Bhagavad Gita* over the last few weeks of the school year. She wanted to plant a seed of inspiration in the children before they left for their summer break from school and from Anna and her energy. Since they all lived on the outskirts of town, it was unlikely that they would meet up at the lakeside park during this time, where she took Anna and Bodhi for daily walks.

The children loved the opening of the story, particularly Amir, who had no doubt anticipated a great battle and a slaughter like something out of one of the *Avengers* movies that he so liked. But, when Arjuna, the leader of the army trying to install his older brother and rightful heir on the throne, was reluctant to pursue this fight against his relatives and the teachers of his youth, he turned to his charioteer, who was revealed as Lord Krishna, for advice. This resulted in a long spiritual discourse, which made Amir quite angry.

"Why doesn't Arjuna just fight them?" he asked.

"Amir, *The Bhagavad Gita* is part of a much longer story called the *Mahabharata*, which has many battles, but this tract is a discourse on how war only shows the conflict within each of us."

"That's stupid," Amir said, quite angrily. "The other *Avengers* would beat up Thor if he talked to them like this."

Maggie spent another fifteen minutes trying to calm Amir and explain the importance of this Hindu biblical text. Finally Anna had had enough of this "discourse," and she twirled her hand and all of them found themselves in the celestial park with Joseph. Debby and Amir cried out in fright.

"It's all right," Anna told them. "This is a park in...heaven, where I talk to my Krishna."

Joseph smiled, and the radiation of love pouring out of him was quieting for the others. "Not quite, my dear." He looked from child to child. "So what do we have here?"

"Oh Joseph, I'm so sorry," Maggie added, quite perplexed by her daughter's precipitous action. "We were discussing *The Bhagavad Gita*, but I wasn't making much headway with Amir, and so Anna transported us here." Maggie turned to her daughter. "Anna, who just can't do that."

"I tired of hearing Amir complaining."

Before Amir who answer back, Joseph turned his attention to him. "Amir, how nice to meet you."

"Who are you? Are you some kind of ghost?"

Joseph smiled. "No, I'm as real as you, but not quite as solid. Come here. You can pinch me if you like."

Daunted, Amir just shook his head. "I believe you."

"So, you were asking why Arjuna didn't just enter the battle and fight his relatives." Amir nodded his head, still somewhat taken aback. "Amir, you have a little sister?"

"Yes. Kashmi."

"And if both you and Kashmi wanted something only one of you could have, would you kill her for it?"

Maggie put a hand to her mouth to stifle a cry.

"No. That's wrong."

"Killing your sister would be like killing yourself?"

Amir thought about this for a moment. "Yes, I guess so."

"And this is what held Arjuna back from killing his own family, and Krishna used this situation, as I believe Ms. Langford has told you, as instruction about how any war is about a war between higher and lower aspects of yourself."

Maybe it was the elevated energy of this dimension, but Amir and the other children seemed to understand Joseph's rather philosophical point more readily.

Amir slowly nodded his head.

"I see great things in your future, Amir, but like all of us, you must first win the battle within yourself."

Joseph twirled his hand, and the children were back in the sitting room of Maggie's home. They were all rather stunned. She immediately brought everybody to their feet and had them go out to the backyard to run off the energy with Bodhi chasing after them.

Maggie would have to talk with Anna about this spontaneous intervention. What if the children told their parents about it and it led to further inquiries from them, especially Amir's father? This exact situation had always frightened her—a premature demonstration of Anna's formidable powers. When the children returned from their afternoon break, Maggie gathered them in the living room. They all sat cross-legged on the floor in their meditative pose.

"I know our little visit to see Joseph in...his realm, may have been shocking, but this is what we would call a conscious dream."

The children nodded their heads. Debby spoke up, "You mean like when I dream of talking with my dead grandpa?"

"Yes, something like that. What you have to understand is that there is more to us and to our reality than most people realize, but I must apologize for this rather abrupt introduction to Anna's...bigger world, which won't happen again." Maggie looked sternly at her daughter.

"Can Joseph throw lightning bolts like Thor?" Amir asked.

"I know there are movies out about super beings from other realms, but the reality of it is far less...extravagant."

"Can he show us how to disappear or walk through walls?" Amir asked, further trying Maggie's patience.

"He would do no such thing, even if he could." She paused for a moment. "In India, the land of your forefathers, there are tales of yogis who have special powers, but they were earned by lifetimes of spiritual dedication and would never be used for selfish purposes or to harm people for any reason."

Amir didn't like this prohibition. "What if aliens came and wanted to kill us all? Wouldn't they fight them?"

"There was a great Indian named Gandhi who choose not to use violence to fight the British who had invaded and taken over his country long ago. He chose instead not to cooperate with their rule, like Martin Luther King did during the civil rights movement here years later, and they both finally won out."

Debby added, "But weren't they killed?"

Maggie nodded her head. "Sometimes that is the karmic debt they take on like Jesus did to elevate all humanity."

"Well, nobody is going to kill me, and if Joseph won't give me powers, I'm going to tell my father and he'll make him."

141

Maggie looked sternly at him. "Go ahead, and you won't be welcomed back to this school."

Amir smirked. "We'll see."

After they were all picked up by their parents, Maggie and Anna took Bodhi for his afternoon walk. At the park Maggie sat on the bench and watched her daughter play with her dog, while she thought about the repercussions of Amir's threat. She had no doubt that this angry little boy would tell his father about Joseph and their trip to see him. The man had been taken aback at his son being taught to meditate. She couldn't imagine his reaction to him being whisked away to a spiritual dimension.

Finally, sensing her mother's despondence, Anna stepped over and sat next to her on the bench.

"I sorry, Mama. But Amir can be so...hard in the head."

Maggie smiled. "It's called hardheaded, my dear."

"Maybe he's not right for our school. Gish and Devi are of higher vibration."

"We'll see."

Amir did not come to school for the last week of the spring semester. A few days later Maggie received a letter from his father telling her that they would be taking Amir to another school for the second grade, but would appreciate a letter from Maggie stating that he had finished the first grade in good standing. She immediately wrote the letter and sent it off, but doubted that this would be the end of it.

Chapter 24

Two weeks later, Maggie and Anna were shopping at the Whole Foods Market on Valley Road south of Laguna Lake when they ran into Amir's mother, Parmita. She immediately stepped over to them in the produce department.

"Maggie, I'm so sorry about Hari pulling our son out of your school."

"I can understand his reaction, if he was at first annoyed at Amir learning to meditate."

Parmita smiled. "Yes, it was a rather shocking story for my husband, if not for me. I would've loved to be transported to this...park in the sky, as Amir called it."

"Parmita, my utmost apologies. Anna went ahead and did it without asking me first, but we've talked and it won't happen again."

The woman squinched her mouth. "Afraid it's too late for Amir. Hari is insistent that we place him in the Montessori Children's School for the remainder of his primary education."

Maggie reached over and took the woman's hand. "It's a good school. I spent a couple days there to learn about their kindergarten approach before I started homeschooling Anna last year."

With the mention of her, they both looked at the unusually quiet Anna standing back and listening to their conversation. This appeared to be her cue. "Amir, very angry boy."

Parmita nodded her head and turned back to Maggie. "He gets it from his father." She lowered her head. "And I don't know what he might do, Maggie. At first he threatened to go to the school authorities, but he seems to have calmed down in the last week." She looked up. "But you should prepare yourself just in case."

"Thanks for the heads-up, Parmita." The woman bowed and

left them to their shopping.

On the drive home, Anna spoke from her car seat. "Maybe time we move to India."

Maggie looked at her daughter in the rearview mirror. "Well, maybe a visit this summer, but I can't promise anything."

Anna closed her eyes, and a moment later she said, "Swami says we welcomed to come."

Maggie smirked. "Oh, did he?" She shook her head. "I'll confirmed that with your father first, but it's a long flight."

Anna shook her head. "My way faster. Could just...move our spirits there."

"But our physical bodies may get hungry after a while."

Anna thought about this prospect for a moment. "Good one, Mom."

That weekend Maggie contacted Thomas's sister Miranda in Washington State and obtained his up-to-date contact information. He was still teaching at Yogi Vinanda's ashram in Chennai, India, on the southeastern coast of the country. The location surprised her; it wasn't a real yoga hotspot, but it was the home of Sri Aurobindo and Sri Ramana's ashrams, two of her favorite Indian yogis. She decided to express-mail him a letter instead of just calling him out of the blue. A week later she received a call from Thomas. He was thrilled that they were thinking of coming to visit him, as was his guru. They decided on a date in early July where it would be less busy at the ashram due to the monsoon season. He also emailed her medical information about updating vaccination shots, which didn't thrill either of them, and the visa requirements. Luckily they had almost a month to prepare.

Fortunately, since Thomas could not help with travel expenses, Maggie had saved the advance from her next children's book for a rainy day or, as it turned out, for a rainy-day visit to India. Apparently some higher part of herself had foreseen that this trip would happen sooner than later. And in her talks with

Thomas, Maggie had made it clear that, while Anna was bound to draw some attention, she didn't want Swami or anybody else to specialize her, and she didn't want any publicity about her child, even in ashram newsletters. Thomas promised to follow her wishes as far as he could, but also said that he wasn't in a position to demand anything of his guru. However, Swami understood the problem, given that he himself had been called a child Buddha, despite being Hindu, that had drawn unwarranted attention, which both he and his parents later regretted.

Days before their flight, Maggie drove to Santa Barbara to leave Bodhi with her parents while they were away. Maggie had booked a round-trip flight, but one where she could change the return date if needed. Grace was pleased that they were going to see Anna's father, but didn't understand why he couldn't come here instead of them making the long trek to India.

"Mom, he's a yoga bum, teaching classes to pay his way at the ashram, making traveling back and forth a real hardship." Her mother didn't state the obvious. Maggie hurriedly added, "And besides I wanted to bring Anna to India, the home of our Hindu faith."

"Where she supposedly has had many past lives, I assume," Grace said rather skeptically.

"Yes, we believe so."

Grace just shook her head. "Well, don't let them deify her quite yet." Maggie gave her mother a questioning look. "As I've said, I can see how everybody in your...community treats her."

Anna came in from the backyard where she had been playing with Bodhi. Grace knelt down. "I'm going to miss you, my dear."

Anna patted her on the arm. "I'll visit you in your dreams, Grandmom."

Grace stood up quickly. "You can just call," she said, recalling her last dream with Anna at their house.

Maggie almost laughed at her mother's adverse reaction to any dreamtime contact.

The next morning Mark drove the three women to the airport in Los Angeles. Grace had decided to drive along with them to forestall her husband pressing Maggie on the support issue he had brought up earlier. When he first heard of her visit, Mark had urged Maggie to have a lawyer draw up papers for Thomas to sign establishing him as Anna's father, which would allow her to use the court system here and in India to petition for support. Maggie unequivocally refused to go along with this plan, and they had not spoken until she drove down to drop off Bodhi. At that point, he suggested she leave her car at the house and he would ferry them back and forth to the airport. Their Cathay Pacific flight was twenty-four hours long including a two-hour layover in Hong Kong, so Maggie wanted to drive to LAX instead of taking a commuter flight there.

The flight to Hong Kong was rather uneventful. Anna had insisted on a window seat so she could see the Arctic ice cap, but the effects of the high altitude had her meditating only hours into the flight. This drew some attention, but the plane was packed with businessmen and tourists who paid little heed to Anna's cross-legged lotus pose, especially when the cabin lights were turned down for sleep time. However, the flight from Hong Kong to Chennai, India, was filled with mostly yoga types on retreat, and by the time they landed the child Buddha already had a following. Some had even called ahead to book any vacancies at the Vinanda Ashram while cancelling their other plans.

Maggie did her best to deflect any inquiries, and after a while even engaged Anna to keep her present. But after clearing customs, a white-clad Indian yogi holding their name sign gathered the two of them and their luggage and whisked them away to an American SUV for the two-hour drive to the ashram. The others took the beat-up ashram van. This was exactly what Maggie had feared—them receiving special treatment—but it would've been worse to protest at this point. She would have another talk with Thomas, and if need be, with Swami about

Anna being treated in this way.

Sensing her mother's distress on the drive to the ashram, Anna put a hand on her mother's arm and quoted Meher Baba's famous dictum, "Don't worry, be happy."

Maggie had a good laugh and gathered up her child and sat Anna on her lap, soaking up her soothing energy. With such a child in hand, how could anything go wrong?

Chapter 25

Their driver, Mesh, called ahead and Thomas was waiting for them on the steps of the ashram's Visitor's Center. As the car drove up, he raced down the wet steps from the afternoon monsoon showers, opened the back door, and picked up Anna while he gave Maggie a half-hug when she stepped out.

"I can't believe you're here," he said, tears rolling down his cheeks.

"Well, I can see why you don't fly back and forth more often."

"Yes, it is a long flight. Hope it wasn't too tiring?"

"Anna meditated some of the way, so she's a lot fresher than me," Maggie added.

Mesh walked over, pulling their luggage bags. "Let's get you settled in, and if you need some time before dinner, you can take a nap."

"I not need sleep," Anna insisted. Her father just smiled back.

Thomas led them along a flat-stone path around the Visitor's Center to a two-story pink motel with long rows of rooms, some with air conditioning units.

"Motel 6?" Maggie said.

"Kind of. We have lots of yoga students staying with us at any one time. We've put you in a downstairs corner unit close to the main hall so you won't have much of a trek."

The room was more spacious than she expected, and Thomas or somebody had decorated it with vases of fresh Angel orchids. "Very nice, Thomas."

"Daddy, where do you stay?" Anna asked.

He put her down and knelt beside his daughter. "I have a small meditation hut where the yogis stay, but it's not far."

"Can I see it?" Anna asked.

"Let's wait until later, Anna." He stood up and turned to Maggie. "So, why don't you take a nap? We've just finished our afternoon meditation, and dinner will be in an hour or so."

"I'll take a shower, but if I lie down you're never getting me up," Maggie said.

"I'm fresh. Don't need a bath. Can go with you, Daddy."

"Anna, we'll have plenty of time together, but first we'll eat and then have a private...session with Swami."

Maggie added, "Yes, dear. Let's follow their schedule. We don't want impose on them." Anna nodded her head and stepped over to the window with its view of the lush garden that surrounded the living quarters. Thomas left, and Maggie immediately unpacked their clothes, put them away in the "distressed painted" but colorful chest of drawers, and stepped into the shower with its new plastic flower curtain and a recently scrubbed floor. When she came out, Anna was meditating in the sea-grass-woven chair next to the bed. She opened her eyes. "Daddy tight. Something is wrong with him."

"Anna. He is a lowly teacher here, and he must abide by Swami's wishes."

"Okay. We let Swami...run the show."

Maggie laughed. "Let's hope it's not too showy."

"But I'm hungry now."

Maggie did lay down for a moment but quickly fell asleep, only to have Thomas shake her awake an hour later. In the bathroom she splashed some water on her face, and they followed him to the banquet hall. It had a cafeteria setup with tables and plastic folding chairs and a buffet line. They stood in line and filled their plates from the wide selection of vegetarian and rice dishes. At the front of the room was a slightly elevated table where Swami sat, and they were ushered to it and directed to take their place on his right side.

Swami, who appeared to be in his mid-sixties and wearing black-framed eyeglasses, bowed to them as they set their trays down. Maggie and Anna bowed back, and he patted the seat next to him for Anna to sit down. Thomas took his place on the other side of his teacher.

"It is nice to finally meet you, Anna...and Maggie. You have such a bright aura, little one."

Anna smiled and said, "Yours white too." She stared at the holy man, then reached over and touched his side.

The holy man shuddered as he closed his eyes, his eyelids twitching. "Oh my," he finally said and opened his eyes.

"I fix kidney thing," she added.

Maggie shook her head. "Anna, what did I tell you about that?"

Swami waved his hand. "No, let Spirit move her, Ms. Maggie." He closed his eyes again. A moment later, he added, "I do have some kidney stones."

"All gone now." Anna looked down at her plate and then up at Swami. "We say grace?"

"Yes, and why don't you say it for us." Thomas clicked his fork against his water glass, and the room went quiet.

Anna bowed her head and repeated the grace said at Ma hi' Ma's Hindu ashram:

The food is One.

We who offer food are One.

The fire of hunger is One.

All action is One

We who know this are One.

Swami raised his head and the others followed. "Thank you, Anna. Your mother has taught you well."

Anna was about to correct him but only nodded her head in agreement, and looked down at her plate and began to eat her dinner. Unlike in the West, everybody mostly ate their meal in relative silence, although Swami did say a few things to Thomas. Afterward Swami gave everybody his blessing, stood up and walked out of the hall. Thomas stepped over to Maggie and Anna. "Swami wants to meditate, and said he will call us when he's ready to meet with you."

"You have a pond with ducks," Anna said.

"Why, yes we do. Would you like to see them?" her father asked.

"We bring bread to feed?" Thomas turned to Mesh who was standing a few feet back. He nodded his head and headed for the kitchen. They walked out of the hall, down another winding flat-stone path to the pond on the east side of the ashram. The sun had set and the path was lit by ankle-high electric lanterns. There were stone benches, and Maggie and Thomas sat down while Anna strolled to the water's edge and sat on the wet grass as the ducks started to paddle over to her.

"I'm really sorry about Anna's impromptu healing. I've asked her repeatedly to ask first, or ask me first."

"I'm sure Swami appreciated it. He has had a problem passing kidney stones." Thomas paused. "Somebody at Ma hi' Ma's ashram sent me the news article about the little boy's recovery from bone cancer in San Luis Obispo. I take it that was Anna?"

Maggie nodded her head. "Well, with Joseph's guidance, we did follow a protocol, and nobody figured it out."

"Joseph?"

"Anna's spirit guide."

"He talks to both of you?" Thomas asked with a half-startled expression.

"Well, occasionally Anna shifts our spirits to his astral park for consultations."

"Oh my," Thomas said. Maggie smiled. He was picking up his guru's expressions. It was endearing.

Mesh came back with a bag of bread crumbs and walked down to the pond handing it to Anna. She quickly opened the bag and began throwing bits of stale bread out onto the moss-covered pond for the ducks to feed. They watched her for a moment. Thomas turned to Maggie. "I need to do something." He waved Mesh over. "Mesh will sit with you until I come back." The yogi nodded his head and took a seat on the bench.

They talked about the ashram, but the yogi deflected any questions about Swami Vinanda's history. Twenty minutes later, after Anna had emptied her bag and had come up to sit with them, Thomas returned.

"I had a talk with Swami. He feels it would be better if the two of you met with him in the morning after meditation."

"Which is what...4:00 a.m.?" Maggie asked hesitantly.

Thomas laughed. "No. In deference to our Western students, it's at 6:00 a.m. But the ashram bell will ring at 5:30, so since it's been such a long day for both of you, I think you should retire for the early-morning riser."

Maggie stood and took her daughter by the hand. "That's sounds better. I'm really exhausted, as you can no doubt tell."

Thomas smiled and escorted them back to their room. He gave Anna a goodnight kiss on the cheek, but merely took Maggie's hands and said, "Good night. Sleep well."

Chapter 26

The morning meditation was quite powerful as Anna's presence permeated the room, or so some of the more attuned could perceive. After Thomas had gathered them from their quarters, he meditated on the raised platform with Swami and the other teachers. Maggie and Anna took places at the back of the room. Afterward a few of the yogis looked over at them curiously. Only two meals were served at the ashram, a light lunch and a full dinner, but the cafeteria provided yogi tea all day long. Thomas brought them there, and they took cups and served themselves from the large urns. They sat down and sipped their tea in silence.

"Something wrong, Daddy?" Anna asked.

He smiled. "Oh no, everything is fine." Anna looked at him with those Buddha eyes. "Okay. I think Swami is a little...taken aback by Anna's energy. He expected a bright-eyed child yogi, not a fully realized seven-year-old master."

Maggie stared at him for a moment. "You told him about our astral visits with Joseph?"

Thomas looked down. "Yes." He paused, then added, "Swami is a very elevated being, but what you've described is another order of being all together. She's like a child Anandamayi Ma."

Anna closed her eyes. "You want me to take Swami to talk with Joseph?"

"No, Anna. I would prefer that you...rein in your siddhis... or powers for now."

Maggie nodded her head thankfully.

"No healings?" she asked.

"In that regard, I believe Swami would welcome healing sessions with some of the older yogis and devotees."

Maggie narrowed her eyes. "Okay, but behind the scenes. I don't want people lining up outside the ashram for healings."

"Well, I'm sure we'll work this out to everybody's satisfaction." Thomas stood up and led them out of the hall over to the glass-domed temple where Swami lived and held his audiences. He was meditating on a raised dais with an ornate gold background of carved saintly figures; there were several decorative pillows laid out for them to sit on. After a while Swami opened his eyes and smiled at them. He motioned for Anna to come up and sit next to him.

Anna looked at her mother who nodded her head. She stepped up and sat on the large rose-colored, embroidered pillow next to Swami, who closed his eyes and soaked up some of the energy. "My dear child, you are a revelation."

Anna bowed her head. "The God within reveals all things."

"Yes, indeed. So tell me of your lineage?"

It took Anna a moment to decipher the word's meaning. "I once Tibetan..."

"Rinpoche," Maggie quietly added, "and Hindu Guru."

"Yes, I can see that in your aura. Maybe, while you're here, you can travel to Nepal where the Tibetans now live."

Anna smiled. "I like warm weather."

Swami laughed. "I see, but you can always warm yourself from within."

"Yes, remember meditating in snow with wet towel and drying it."

Swami looked at Maggie. "So she has total recall?"

Anna answered for herself. "I not like think of past. This moment all there is."

"Yes, indeed, young Anna." He closed his eyes, again drawing in the energy emanating from her. He opened his eyes. "I am most pleased that you have come, and would like you to consider our ashram as your second home."

"With Daddy here, it is."

Swami looked at Thomas and nodded his head. He closed his eyes and touched his fingers in his meditation mudra. Thomas motioned for Anna to step down from the dais. All three bowed their heads and backed out of the temple chamber.

After several days adjusting to the flow of ashram life, taking yoga classes where Anna impressed the yogis with her asana-pose mastery and doing group meditations, Mesh drove the three of them to Ramana Maharshi's ashram. It was located south of Chennai at the foot of Mount Arunachala where the famed yogi had lived for years. While her mother had read her stories about the Hindu saint, Anna could feel his energy here which some claimed still permeated the ashram and nearby mountain where he had meditated in its caves. Touring the bookstore and temple and walking around the grounds, Anna told her parents, "I like Rama. He not tell people what to do. He just meditate and let his energy do talking."

Thomas laughed. "Yes, he wasn't known for his discourses but for the power of his silent presence."

Anna nodded her head. "That is kind of teacher I want to be."

Thomas was somewhat taken aback. "So you've already planned on a ministry?"

Anna gave her father a rather indulgent look. "I plan to meditate like Rama, and what happens…happens."

Thomas looked at Maggie. "I sensed the beginning of her spiritual unfolding on my visit last time, but never suspected it would be this soon."

Maggie shook her head and forced a smile. "Me either."

The next day, while further familiarizing themselves with the ashram, Maggie and Anna stepped into their small medical dispensary. An old yogi in a loincloth lay on the table while an Indian doctor poked his side and stomach for pain reactions. Before Maggie could stop her, Anna stepped over and placed her hand under the right side of the yogi's abdomen. His body shook, and after a while he took a deep sigh of relief and relaxed. He turned his head to look at the little miracle-worker.

"Eat too much sugar, bad for vine thing."

The Indian didn't speak English, but the doctor did and understood her reference, and translated it for him. Dr. Khatri turned back to them. "Like I've been telling him, his pancreas is, or was, getting worse."

The grouchy old yogi said something back to him. Maggie and Anna looked to the doctor. "He says he prefers the girl's sweet energy to my poking."

Khatri said something to him and told them, "I'll run some tests, and we'll see what they show."

The yogi sat up on the table, and the doctor translated. He shook his head and said something. "He says he's cured," the doctor said tentatively.

Blood tests taken the next day confirmed that the yogi's early-stage pancreatic cancer, the most difficult type to treat, showed early signs of remission. The yogi's colleagues, who were expecting the worst news, were lined up outside Anna's room the next morning. Thomas told them to go to meditation, and he would talk with Swami and the girl's mother about healing sessions.

Later in Swami's temple, a very upset mother was refusing to let her daughter conduct wholesale healings for the ashram's sick. Anna patiently sat and listened to their back-and-forth argument. Swami turned to Thomas. "You're the child's father. Don't you have a say?"

Thomas looked down. "Swami, I've told you, in name only. Maggie is her legal guardian, and I must defer to her wishes." Swami Vinanda gave Thomas a withering look.

Anna finally raised her hand, and the room went quiet. She sat in meditation for a long moment, before she opened her eyes. "Joseph says, if I can help, I should, but only very ill yogis. No family or other people."

Swami asked, "Joseph?"

"Her spirit guide," Thomas added.

Swami and Thomas then looked to Maggie. "Okay, what can

I say to that, but strictly along these lines, and no camera phones allowed."

"Yes, I know that better than most about a child's premature notoriety," Swami added more evenhandedly, "but Ms. Maggie you must understand that Anna has a mission to fulfill."

Maggie bowed her head. "Yes, Swami, but according to St. Luke, even Jesus didn't start his ministry until he was thirty years old."

Swami smiled. "But we really don't know happened in the years between."

Anna volunteered, "Nobody get sick around boy Jesus."

"There you have it," Swami said with an authoritative gesture. "Let the child choose her path."

Maggie would defer and allow these healings for now, but unlike Swami she was not convinced the timing was right for her daughter to "reveal" herself.

Dr. Khatri selected twelve of his sickest patients. Over the next three days, after morning meditation, Anna and Khatri treated patients in the clinic and they were thoroughly screened for listening devices and cameras. By the end of three days, Anna had outright healed or greatly mitigated a host of serious illnesses from cancer to heart disease. However, word got around about the amazing child healer from America, and local reporters were at their gates within days. Mesh and some of the strong-armed yogis stood outside the closed gates to the ashram and kept them at bay, but more than a few relatives of the cured shared the miracles happening daily at the ashram clinic. Stories with photos of Anna walking the grounds of the ashram soon made the headlines of the local papers, and before long reporters from national newspapers and tabloids were descending on Chennai.

Maggie decided that they had to leave India and changed their return flight plans. Swami thought she was overreacting, but while Anna wanted to stay longer, she could see her mother's great distress and went along with these plans. Swami agreed to use his influence to quash any further news inquiries. Three days later, in the dead of night, Mesh and Thomas snuck Maggie and Anna out of the ashram and drove them to the airport for a late-night flight back to Los Angeles.

"Maggie, I'm so sorry about all of this. We should've listened to you. You've been managing Anna quite well so far."

She reached over to hold Thomas's hand. "Anna did get permission from Joseph, so I must assume this is part of some grander plan. Don't blame yourself, and in a year or two we'll return and maybe for a much longer stay."

"Let's keep in touch. I've been planning on returning to the United States to set up a Kundalini Yoga practice, so a return trip may not be needed." He paused. "And I won't be under any constraints there." Maggie realized this referred to Swami's insistence on celibacy at the ashram.

"What about Swami? How will all this sit with him?"

"He's been thinking of doing a tour of the United States, and I'm sure Southern California will now be on his schedule."

Anna was heartbroken to leave her father this soon, but she knew from her mother's earlier entreaty not to "grab hold" of his energy field, and to allow her father to find his own way back to them. On the return flight, they both slept more and later Maggie read Anna children's stories about the lives of Hindu saints from a book that Swami had presented to them on their departure.

Chapter 27

They were picked up at LAX in the early morning by Maggie's parents. They had a six-hour layover in Hong Kong, and lost a calendar day crossing the international dateline. She had emailed them from India on their change of plans with a new arrival time, and once they landed she called her mother who said that they would be waiting for them outside the airport's luggage pickup. It took an hour to walk through the huge airport and gather up their three suitcases, but after another heads-up call, her father's blue Subaru Outback was waiting at the curb for them. He helped load their luggage, gave her and Anna quick hugs, and they were off into LA's early- morning traffic.

Grace turned around in her front seat and immediately asked Maggie with a coy smile, "Why the change of plans?"

"Can we talk about it when we get back to Santa Barbara?"

"Okay. So how did you like southern India? Was it hot?"

"Very hot, Grandma, and it rain every day," Anna volunteered.

"Was it nice to see your daddy again?"

"He good yogi, and his Swami is very good yogi."

Without looking over his shoulder, Mark asked, "I guess you didn't ask about support?"

"No. The subject never arose, but he does plan to return to California and set up a yoga practice, and we'll see how that turns out."

Her father just shook his head and pulled onto the entranceway to the 405 freeway heading north.

Maggie did tell them about Vinanda's ashram, their visit to the ashram of Ramana Maharshi south of the city, but since none of this interested her parents very much, the conversation switched to updates about their life and her sister Jill and her family, and of course Bodhi's stay with them.

"I don't know what you feed him, but he's the most mild-mannered dog I've ever been around," Grace said. "On our walks to the park or along the beach, when we would meet up with other dogs, there was none of the male sniffing or territorial growling. The other dogs just wanted to follow him around."

"Well, Mother. Bodhi is short for Bodhisattva." Her father snickered at this explanation.

"This Bodhi's last life as dog," Anna added. "He come back as a human next time."

"Let's hope he'll be better at providing for his family than some humans."

Maggie and her mother ignored his sarcastic remark.

"He come back as my little brother," Anna said, much to her mother's surprise.

Grace turned around and stared at her daughter, but didn't ask the obvious question. After dinner that night, Maggie and her mother sat out on the patio sipping iced teas and watching the day turn to night. "So, what caused the quick exit?"

"Let's leave it at: Anna's energy and healing ability caused a minor sensation."

Grace smirked. "Oh, really." She reached for the cultural section of a recent daily *Los Angeles Times* and handed it to her daughter. The headline of the short news brief read: *America Girl Heals Whole Ashram of Indians.*

Maggie quickly read the article, which didn't mention either of them by name. "At least they didn't get a name."

"But, my dear, that's only a matter of time. You did fly with passports and visas, and bureaucrats everywhere are subject to bribes."

Maggie closed her eyes. A moment later Anna came out carrying her mother's cell phone with Bodhi trailing behind her. "You get call soon." Grace shook her head, and then arched her eyebrows when the phone chimed a moment later.

She took it from her daughter. Saw the caller ID, and put her finger up for Grace to give her a minute. While Maggie stepped away from the patio and into the backyard, Anna jumped up on her grandmother's lap, while Bodhi lay down beside her chair. Maggie could hear her mother asking about "healing all those people in India."

"So, Maggie," Ma hi' Ma said, "I hear you had an eventful trip to India."

"Wow. That's fast. I assumed you'd learn about the trip from the local devotees, but as to eventful..."

"As you know, my dear, the yogi grapevine is just as pervasive as many others, and everybody is abuzz about the 'seven-year-old America yogi master and healer,' if I may quote a source."

Maggie shook her head in dismay. "Well, that may be the least of our problems."

"Really. If I recall, people lined up outside your house asking for healings was a real concern of yours."

Maggie proceeded to tell Guru about Anna's astral field trip and the harsh reaction from one of her student's fathers and the threats he had made about protesting to the school board. This was followed by a more detailed account of what happened in India. "I'll need to call James, and I think it best that you plan on driving up here this week. It's only a month until school starts, which doesn't give James much time to...fix this."

"Oh Ma, thank you so much. I knew I could count on you." They made plans for her and Anna to meet James at the ashram the coming weekend.

When Maggie walked back to the patio, her mother and Anna had gone inside and were eating bowls of strawberry ice cream. Maggie went back to the kitchen and scooped out a bowl for herself. She joined them in the living room.

"Important call?" Grace asked.

"Well, the word has gotten around, and Ma hi' Ma wants us to consult with the ashram's lawyer."

Grace nodded her head. "That may not be a bad idea. We don't want to subject young Anna to too much public scrutiny, I would imagine."

"Yes, Mother. That wouldn't be good."

Grace looked down at her granddaughter. "And thank you, Anna, for healing me of cancer." She turned to Maggie. "I assume she was the source of my miraculous recovery?"

Anna looked up at her grandmother and added rather ingeniously, "Babies have great energy."

The next day they drove home, and Maggie picked up her mail from the post office hold. There was an envelope from the San Luis Coastal Unified School District. She quickly opened it. Inside was a letter from Mrs. Linden, whom she had met with for her homeschooling certification, which had now "come under question," and that she needed to call and set an appointment to discuss "serious complaints about the nature of her home school and her daughter's...psychological status."

She immediately drove to the local FedEx store and faxed a copy of the letter to the ashram, for them to forward to James Edwards. They stopped by the Whole Foods store to replenish their food supply. At home there was several phone messages from Mrs. Linden, each one more strident than the next. Maggie called the woman, apologized for her late response, told her they had been out of the country and had just returned, and set up a meeting with her in three weeks. Linden wanted it sooner, but Maggie said she had to consult with the lawyer who had set up her homeschooling program.

"A lawyer?" she asked.

"Yes, James Edwards from San Francisco. I had mentioned his name on my last visit, and that he looks after the legal concerns of Sri Ma hi' Ma's Hindu devotees."

"Oh, I see. But this may...complicate matters."

Maggie tried to contain her anger. "Well, you are the one who questioned my child's 'psychological status.'"

Linden quickly ended the conversation and had her secretary set up the meeting. Later, Edwards called from San Francisco and asked that Maggie and her daughter drive up for a meeting with him in two days. She was told to bring contact information on all her students, past and present, and for the ashram in India where they had stayed on their recent visit. Shortly afterward, Ma called and said she had talked with James, and that the matter required urgent attention and that after meeting with him, she needed to drive up to the ashram for the weekend to "complete the process." Her guru wouldn't fill her in any further.

Maggie fixed a late lunch for the two of them and put out Bodhi's food, and they all took a walk to the park afterward. There were a few children playing, and Anna said hello to her friends and explained her long absence and they played together for a while. Maggie sat on the bench lost in thought. She understood why James Edwards would want contact information on his students and the Indian ashram. He would no doubt overnight the parents affidavits to fill out attesting to the quality of the education their children were receiving, but she assumed the "process" that Ma needed "to complete," had something to do with Swami Vinanda. Since it was time for her daughter's nap, she collected Anna and Bodhi and walked back to their house.

Anna could sense her mother's distress. "They want to make me Swami Anna."

Maggie nodded her head. "Of course. To deflect any inquiry about your healing ability and…more." She remembered having this conversation with Joseph and Ma, and him explaining why he wanted Anna to be free of any official status, but things had changed. At home after Anna's nap, Maggie told her daughter, "I think we need to talk with Joseph."

"Goody. I miss him." Without further ado, she twirled her raised hand, and they found themselves in his celestial park where it was always sunny and clear, and Joseph was always sitting on the bench dressed the same.

"To answer your first question, Maggie. I don't live here. This is a projection from my real…abode."

Anna looked at her mother. "I tell Ma hi' Ma, but she say wait to tell you."

Maggie laughed. "Yes, I seem to be low woman on the totem pole."

Anna didn't get the reference but let it go.

"Anna is correct. Ma and the lawyer feel the best way to protect Anna's...spiritual manifestations is to initiate her as a Hindu swamini."

"Which you earlier opposed."

"Yes, but things change and a new perspective may be needed." Joseph paused to allow Maggie time to adjust. "Again, we of this realm are sometimes amazed by human behavior, or I should say the general lack of acceptance of Spirit and its manifestations."

"Well, I can understand Mr. Kumar's reaction to his son being whisked away to this realm."

Joseph nodded his head. "Yes, an oversight on my part as well, but we need to seriously consider Mr. Edwards's point of view and how to...work the system, as I believe you say."

"So, you think we should go along with him and Ma, and let them initiate Anna?"

Joseph smiled and turned to Anna. "What say you, Anna?"

She thought for a moment. "I want to heal people, and if this opens the way, okay. But I not be like Swami V or Ma and sit on throne like queen."

Joseph turned to Maggie. "So, it seems like you need to have some...straight talk with Ma hi' Ma."

She adamantly added, "Yes, and the first of many, including our Mrs. Linden and the school authorities, or so I assume."

Joseph smiled. "God help them."

Chapter 28

The next day Maggie called her publisher Jean Millburn and said she was coming to San Francisco and needed to stop by and talk with her about matters that may affect the publicity on her new children's book. Jean was intrigued and asked for more information, but Maggie said it would be best to discuss this in person. She asked if Maggie would be bringing her co-author, Bodhi, and if so, she would have some treats ready for him. This lightened the mood, and she thanked Jean for this consideration, and said she would bring him. Maggie also kept a keen eye on her daughter to see if this dispute affected her in any way. But, as always, Anna easily maintained her remarkable spiritual equilibrium that was unruffled by the human conflicts around her. Maggie decided that meditating with her daughter might help her smooth out her own concerns and their rather ragged expression. She did that the next day, but realized that while it may have "polished" her aura a bit, it didn't seep down into the core of her being so readily. She would have to do the spiritual heavy-lifting herself. It did, however, give her further insight into Anna's healing of others, or how it was a two-way street. Maybe she wasn't as receptive as she could be.

So they headed out on Thursday, just another grand adventure for Anna and Bodhi, but one in which Maggie couldn't help but feel apprehensive about its effects on their lives. In Mountain View they parked on the street in front Millburn Press and stepped inside with Bodhi trailing after them. As a bestselling author, Maggie and her entourage were enthusiastically greeted by the staff. As they walked down the hall to Jean's second-floor office, she noticed the covers of her last two books prominently displayed on the wall with glowing *New York Times* reviews framed under them.

Jean stepped out into the hall to greet them and show them

inside. They were escorted to their chairs and Bodhi to his rug and bowl of treats. Jean noticed that Bodhi looked to Anna before devouring them; this young girl seemed to be in communication with her dog. *How remarkable*, she thought. Jean knew that Anna had inherited her mother's artistic talents and could only hope that extended to literary skills as well. But first things first, as she showed Maggie, and as it turned out, both Anna and Bodhi, the suggested covers for *The Dog Who was God*. There was a back-and-forth discussion on the merits of the cover mockups, but in the end Maggie consulted with Anna, who seemed to conduct her own exchange with Bodhi, and they all came to a decision: they liked the more graphic design over the strictly pictorial cover with its dog image.

"Use Bodhi's picture, and we like it better," Anna volunteered.

Jean could only shake her head over this most unusual collaboration. "Well, I could have Barry substitute his dog picture in that design."

Maggie shook her head. "No. That won't be necessary. It's an abstract concept, and more the pictorial you make it, the more people will take it literally and judge it as such."

"My feelings exactly," Jean added.

Anna paused for a moment. "People here take things wrong. I like India better; people there more...spiritual."

"Yes. You've just come back from there. Tell me about it?" Jean asked.

Maggie paused.

"Or, we could just go onto the...publicity issue you mentioned."

"Well Jean, they're both tied together," Maggie said. She paused again. "But, let me add that I haven't been completely forthright about my daughter's...development, and it seems that it has come back to bite us on the ass."

Anna laughed, turned to Bodhi, and he barked. "Good one, Mom."

"You ready for this?" Maggie said, shaking her head.

Jean sat back in her chair intrigued but cautious. "Go ahead, Maggie. I've been anticipating such a talk for a while."

Maggie looked at her questioningly, but didn't wait for a further explanation. "Anna was born totally awakened, which means she knows her past lives, is not only in communication with spiritual beings of the highest order but travels with them in spirit to other realms."

This was more than Jean had anticipated. She nodded her head tentatively. "Go on."

"This has not been...let's say, exposed, until recently. But unfortunately Anna took my students and me on a 'field trip' to visit her guide in what some would call an astral park."

Jean nodded her head, but unconsciously grabbed the arm of her chair as if to forestall any quick exit to this "park." "And of course, this got back to their parents and then to the school board."

"Exactly, and why I have a meeting later today with my guru's attorney."

The publisher sighed in relief. "I hope he can exert some influence and keep this quiet."

"Well, there's more. While in India visiting her father, she healed a yogi of pancreatic cancer, and many others in the ashram lined up and were healed."

Jean put her hand to her mouth. "Oh my. And I assume the press got wind of it?"

Maggie took the *Los Angeles Times* article out of her purse and passed it to Jean. She quickly read it. "And of course, this just ups the stakes for the school board and what they are exposing the fine children of San Luis Obispo to."

Maggie nodded her head. "One would assume that they don't want a media circus as well, but we're not sure how this will play out."

Jean looked at her watch. "Let's take an early lunch. I need a drink."

Maggie laughed. "That's two of us."

"What about Bodhi?" Anna asked. He barked and she looked at him, then back to Jean. "He stay here if it all right."

Jean just shook her head at this implied communication. "Of course. I'll have a bowl of water brought in and Barry can walk him if need be."

Anna nodded her head. "Bodhi 'tell me,' if need pee-pee walk and you call blond man from eating place."

Jean just shook her head, stood up, and turned to Maggie. "We may need a pitcher of margaritas."

"Only one drink for me. I still need to drive into San Francisco after lunch."

"Yes, and be alert for your meeting with said attorney."

Maggie nodded and the three of them stepped out for lunch.

At lunch and after a few margaritas, Jean explained the old publishing precept: there's no such thing as bad publicity. Only time would tell the nature of the school system's pushback and what, if anything, needed to be done in regard to her author's new notoriety. But all things being considered, she still thought they should delay the release of the book until after the New Year.

"Hopefully by then things will have cooled down, but I don't think you should take Anna on the publicity jaunt," Jean said.

Anna made a face and then broke out into a smile. "We stay with Grandma, take walks on the beach." She closed her eyes. "Bodhi say he like that."

Jean looked at Maggie and again shook her head at the girl's apparent telepathic communication with her dog, then poured herself another margarita.

In San Francisco James Edwards had been alerted that there was a third member of Ms. Langford's entourage, and a dog walker met them in the lobby of the office building, and after making her acquaintance with Bodhi, took him to the a nearby park for some exercise. Maggie wasn't sure about Mr. Edwards's law practice; she wondered if a lawyer with spiritual leanings would have a small private practice, but discovered on their arrival that this was far from the case. James was a partner in one of San Francisco's most prestigious law firms, if it was peopled by a few reformed hippies from the 1960s flower movement here, Edwards being the most prominent. They took an elevator to the fifteenth floor and were ushered into the man's well-appointed corner office.

Edwards was in his late sixties, a tall slender man with thinning gray hair, wire-rimmed glasses, and a muscular built, no doubt from years of yoga exercise. He came around the table to greet them, shaking Maggie's hand, and squatted to look Anna in the eyes to greet her. She jumped into his arms as if he were a long-lost uncle. This brought tears to his eyes. He stood and moved them over to a sofa setting. He had tea and juice brought in, and they sat across from each other for a long moment.

"I'm awfully sorry, Maggie, that the expression of Anna's advanced spirituality has brought you to my doorstep, but be assured that this firm takes the protection of her...religious rights very seriously, and will not stand for any infringement of them."

"Thank you, James, if I may call you that." Edwards nodded his head. "I've always known that at some point in Anna's development this would be an issue if we stayed in America. I just wasn't prepared for it to happen this soon."

Anna spoke up. "It's God's plan, not anybody else's."

"Okay, and so I'll lay out my plan, and both of you tell me how it sits with you and God."

Neither of them replied, so James went forward to outline it. First, they were gathering the paperwork to turn Maggie's home school into a certified Hindu religious school, which would protect its religious instruction and any advanced spiritual practices. Part of this process would be securing affidavits from the parents of the current students to attest to their satisfaction with their children's education, even from Mr. Kumar who had raised the objections about his son's unauthorized "little visit" to see Anna's spirit guide. Edwards asked, "I take it that he was otherwise pleased with his son's education?"

"Yes, I believe so. Be sure to put the names of both parents on the request since his mother opposed Amir being taken out of my home school."

Edwards made a notation on his iPad. "Second, and of course subject to both of your approvals, Ma would initiate Anna as a full-fledged Hindu swamini, backed up by Swami Vinanda's own affidavit as to her suitability, even at this young age, to be so initiated."

"Don't want to shave head," Anna said.

"No, my dear. As you can see, Ma and her monks and nuns are very Western in their deportment."

"I assume this is to cover any demonstrations of her healing and siddhis, or powers?" Maggie asked. Edward nodded his head. "But," Maggie continued, "we're not going to move to the ashram."

Edwards shook his head. "However, Anna will need to spend time there every summer for the next few years to continue her formal Hindu education, as well as you as a teacher of Hinduism, even if Anna is more advanced than the other devotees there."

"We understand." Maggie looked at Anna who just smiled back at them. "And as to the concern about Anna's...psychological status?"

"Yes. I've been talking with Dr. Marsha Singh, a psychiatrist who specializes in the care and, I might say, protection of the 'spiritually elevated.' She has a practice in Berkeley and has agreed to examine Anna tomorrow, will put her through a series of standard tests, and when she is satisfied, which I'm sure will be the case, she'll certify and testify if needed as to your daughter's...'psychological fitness.'"

Maggie reached over and took a sip of tea. "James, I'm most impressed, not only with your plan but the speed at which you've put this all together."

"While Anna is a fairly advanced spiritual adept, we have had other cases to prepare us for such invasive inquiries from the spiritually less attuned."

Anna smiled and clapped her hands. "You very smart man. You guru in past life in India." Anna gazed at him more closely as if reading the man's spiritual CV in his aura. "Many times, I see." She sat back. "And good health. Keep up daily yoga practice."

James Edwards bowed his head. "I will, Swamini Annananda."

They all laughed, and then James collected Maggie's contact information for her students and the ashram in India, and set up the interview with Dr. Singh in the morning.

Chapter 29

After leaving Bodhi with the firm's unofficial dog sitter for the weekend, Maggie and Anna checked into a nearby hotel for the night. The next morning they drove across the Oakland Bay Bridge from San Francisco to Dr. Singh's office in Berkeley for their 10:00 a.m. appointment. Maggie was a bit alarmed to discover that the good doctor had offices in the mammoth Behavior Health Center, south of the UC Berkeley campus. While attending school there, she had visited stressed-out friends who had been admitted to the Center's psyche ward for drug abuse or bi-polar disorders. But, she trusted James Edwards's handling of their somewhat unusual crisis, and would give Dr. Singh the benefit of the doubt.

They parked their car and entered the concrete-faced multistory building on Dwight Way and took the elevator to Singh's office. Upon stepping into the waiting room, some of her anxiety was dispelled by the Indian music, the sweet smell of incense, and the offer of yogi tea by the receptionist. She was handed a registration sheet and a pre-patient psychological review form to fill out on her daughter. They took a seat in the waiting room, and Maggie started answering the questionnaire. She noticed that the insurance and payment block was marked N/A. Anna just sat there sipping her tea and being quiet. There was one other patient waiting in the room, a hyperactive teenager with his stressed-out mother, or so she assumed. Thirty minutes after Maggie had filled out both forms and handed them back to Vivian, the blond-haired receptionist ushered them into Dr. Singh's office.

Marsha Singh was in her late fifties, short but buxom, her skin lighter than most native East Indians, but definitely a daughter of that country. She glanced up from Maggie's questionnaire forms, squinting over the top of her thin black-framed glasses.

She stood and stepped around her desk to greet them.

"Ms. Langford, Anna, it's wonderful to finally meet the two of you."

She shook hands with Maggie and like James Edwards, Marsha squatted to exchange eye-to-eye contact with Anna. "My dear, I am so sorry that your siddhis have been called into question."

Anna smiled and looked intently at the doctor but didn't respond. Dr. Singh stood up and had them sit in the chairs set out in front of her desk, Anna's with a booster chair in it.

"I've had extensive talks with James and Sri Ma hi' Ma, my own guru, and understand the situation somewhat, but it's always good to get a firsthand account." Maggie nodded her head. "So Anna, I am told that you have a spirit guide, Joseph, and that you are able to shift yourself and others into his presence in" — she glanced down at her notes, then looked back up at Anna — "some kind of astral park setting."

"Yes, but just our spirit bodies. You like to go there?"

Singh wasn't at all alarmed by this suggestion. "Yes, but not now." She turned to Maggie. "I need to evaluate your daughter objectively, and such an exhibition could be taken by others as a kind of subjective psychic contamination."

Maggie nodded her head. "Which is what the other side will no doubt claim she does to others."

"Yes, I believe that may be their position, Maggie — if I can call you that?" She nodded her head. "But, let me ask Anna, when was the first time you visited Joseph there?"

"I, in my crib, not able to talk yet. Very hard. There I in spirit body and…older."

"I see." Singh turned to Maggie. "I've been told by Ma that the two of you were also transported there and can both attest to the validity of this experience?"

"Many times for me," Maggie added.

Singh nodded her head. "Well, I must admit that in my forty

years dealing with people's spiritual experiences, I've never come across such a display of...spiritual prowess, I guess you could call it. I mean, in India you hear of yogis who can bilocate, levitate, and whatnot, but from a strictly Western psychological perspective, this would be inconceivable to most."

Maggie leaned forward in her chair. "But not to you, I hope."

Dr. Singh shook her head. "No, not in the least. I have personally had such experiences in the dream state, but from a strictly conscious point of view, it does blur the lines."

Anna smiled. "Everything one anyway."

Singh chuckled. "Yes, my dear, but most people prefer a discrete separation of their...realities."

"Or, what Joseph says, until...mind let go," Anna said.

"Yes, but the premature...letting go of the mind by some fills this hospital's psyche wards," Singh said.

"And what the educators and their doctors might feel has happened to Anna and would happen to others exposed to her," Maggie said.

Dr. Singh sat back in her chair. "That is very astute, Maggie." She paused. "Yes, but we must understand their concerns, not dismiss them outright, and just claim religious superiority."

Maggie nodded her head. "Yes, of course. So, where do we start?"

"We need to run a series of standardized tests to determine if Anna's advance spiritual practices have affected her emotional stability, or made her in any way delusional or...sorry to say, psychotic, and verify that her mental development has been unaffected." She paused, but seeing Maggie's concern, added, "None of which I'm sure is the case here."

"And if cleared, it may make the case that exposure to her and her practices will not be harmful to others."

Dr. Singh nodded her head again. "Yes, but I believe, to assuage their concerns, that Anna like any spiritual master must use her powers...more discretely."

Anna said, "Yes, Doctor. You right. I wrong to take class to see Joseph, even he say so."

"That's a good start, Anna. I think we'll make quick work of this, and that by the end of the day, I'll have all I need to make my case."

"Okay, let's do it," Maggie said somewhat relieved and impressed by the doctor as well.

Maggie and Anna were taken to a conference room with a long table, where an associate psychologist, Dr. David Shaw, a studious-looking man in his early thirties with lightly shaded eyeglasses, sat down across from them and handed Maggie the first of many questionnaires. When he didn't stand up and leave, Maggie asked, "So you're staying?"

"Yes, after you've finished filling out the parental questionnaire, I need to ask questions of Anna directly."

Maggie nodded her head. "Yes, of course."

The first questionnaire was in regard to her assessment of Anna's moods and if she ever had emotional outbursts, became dejected and sullenly withdrawn, or ever acted impulsively. There were some fifty questions along this line, but Maggie was able to quickly to check them off since Anna had such an even temperament. There were a few more questionnaires that went deeper into her own assessment of Anna's emotional stability, but were just as easy for her to answer. Dr. Shaw read over and graded each questionnaire as she finished it. Then, it was time for him to ask Anna a few questions.

David picked up the next questionnaire to fill out himself and asked, "Anna, do you ever feel sad?"

"Yes, when I see how people suffer."

"Does that make you feel hopeless?"

"No. I know all people come back to God in the end."

David looked up from the form and studied her for a moment, and then made a notation. "Are you sometimes frustrated when others don't share your beliefs?"

Anna shook her head. "No. Everyone say same thing in own words."

David continued along this line for another dozen questions, and when he was finished, picked up another questionnaire. He stared at her for a long moment. "Anna, do you see things that are not there?"

Anna smiled. "I see things that are there but others can't see."

David chuckled. "Yes, of course. Very good." He paused, then went on to the next question. "Are you able to talk with and interact with...nonmaterial beings?"

It took Anna a moment to decipher this question. "Yes, I do."

"When did this...interaction start?"

"When I was a small baby."

David looked over at Maggie, who only nodded her head. "Okay. Do you sometimes wish you could stay with them and not come back?"

"Yes, but I miss Mommy and Bodhi, and I like it here. The sun is warm on your skin, the wind blows through your hair, and there is ice cream."

David chuckled again. "Yes, let's not forget ice cream." He looked down at the next questionnaire and up at Anna. "Okay, now for a few hard questions."

Anna smiled. "I like answer questions."

"Good, Anna." David paused. "If someone tried to hurt your mother, what would you do?"

Anna felt her way through this quagmire of a question. "I send them so much love, they not harm anybody."

"But, what if that didn't work and they still tried to harm her?"

"I step between, die instead, because I know this body not me." David nodded his head. "Or, we run away very fast, and not make bad karma for them."

"But you would not...stop them in any way?" he asked tentatively.

"Not good to…"

Maggie added, "Interfere?"

"Yes, Mama. To interfere with people's…free will, or so says Joseph?"

"Joseph?"

"My spirit guide."

David let out a sigh and then sat back in his chair. He turned to Maggie. "I've been testing children for years, and your daughter is…no child, more like the Dali Lama in a child's body."

"Well, let's not tell the school board that, or they'll think you've been…psychically contaminated, as I believe Dr. Singh cautioned."

David nodded his head and continued with even harder questions for a while longer, and then he administered a child's IQ test, which, after he graded it, he could only shake his head in astonishment. They finished after three hours, and Maggie was told to take a lunch break, and when they came back, Dr. Singh would talk with her. There was a Nepali/Indian restaurant within walking distance, and they went there for lunch. When they finished and returned to Dr. Singh's office, Anna was able to take a nap in the children's break room. Maggie sat in the doctor's waiting room while she finished reviewing Anna's test results and Dr. Shaw's notes.

After fifteen minutes, Dr. Singh stuck her head out the door and waved Maggie inside. Her receptionist was apparently on her lunch break. Maggie noticed boxes of half-eaten Chinese takeout on a nearby table. After they were seated, Singh looked up with a big smile on her face. "Maggie, was your daughter's IQ ever tested?"

"Well, no, since she's been outside the school system."

"She has a 140 IQ, or thereabouts. It's more difficult to ascertain with children, given their limited language skills, but both David and I feel that this is a fair assessment."

"But, I thought the problem here was ascertaining her

emotional stability."

"Yes, of course, and she passed those tests with flying colors. High scores in all areas, and not a thing to concern you or anybody else about, but you have to realize that intelligence is the holy grail of any school system, and evidence of it will make...personal eccentricities more acceptable."

"So, we have an ace in the hole."

"Yes, I feel we do, but when you return home, I'd like you to take Anna to a child psychologist and have them administer an independent IQ test, but only that."

Maggie nodded her head. "I understand. So, what's next?"

"Well, we have what we need at this end to make our case and file a report for James Edwards, and so you're free to leave and drive up to the ashram. I'm sure Ma has plans to add another layer of religious protection for young Anna. If you're staying the whole weekend, I may come up to soak up more of her wonderful energy."

"That would be nice, doctor." Maggie paused. "I see on the form that your services aren't being billed?"

"Oh, James was going to pay for it, but it's my pleasure to be of any assistance to you and your daughter...anytime."

Anna stepped into the office rubbing her eyes. Singh walked around and knelt down to greet her. "Have a nice nap?"

She nodded her head, then reached out and took the woman's hand and gave her a charge of energy that she would never forget. "Payment in full," Singh would later tell James Edwards.

Chapter 30

It was late afternoon on a Friday, and so Maggie decided to start driving to the ashram to beat some of the city's evening rush-hour traffic. Fortunately they were heading north, not west to San Francisco, or east to Sacramento, but they did get caught up in the traffic on Interstate 80 heading to the Six Flags Amusement Park. Once they turned off onto Route 29, they were slowed down somewhat by local traffic but were able to reach Napa Valley by 6:30, where they stopped for dinner. While the ashram was only twenty-five miles north of here, the evening meal would be over by now and Maggie didn't want to impose on them. There was a vegetarian restaurant here that the devotees would sometimes drive to on the weekends, and they stopped there for soup and salads. While they were finishing up, Maggie received a call from Guru.

"Maggie, are we seeing you this evening?"

"Yes, Ma. We're in Napa Valley just finishing up dinner, and should be there in forty minutes."

"Very well. I've had your room prepared, but would like to see you before you retire for the evening."

"Yes Ma, of course."

"I'll have Prema keep an eye out for you. Until then."

When they arrived, Prema escorted them to see Ma in the temple room. She was sitting in meditation with several of her attendants, but could sense the shift of energy in the room when Anna stepped inside. She opened her eyes and held her arms open for Anna to rush up and jump onto her lap. The others stood, bowed in homage, and left.

"My little bundle of bliss."

"That's me, Ma. Annananda, bliss supreme."

Ma shook her head and glanced down at Maggie seated cross-legged on a pillow. "How do you keep things from her?"

"Well, James did mention the name, and of course we know Ananda is Hindu for bliss or happiness."

Ma looked down at Anna. "So, you are fine with becoming a Swamini?"

"Joseph say follow guide of those sent to nurture my... unfolding." Ma nodded her head.

Maggie asked, "What kind of ceremony are you planning?"

"I've talked with James, and he feels that the *bibidisa*, or the full ceremony, is needed." Ma paused for a moment and then continued, "Know that this is a death ceremony, or death to one's old self, and will include the fire ritual, a kind of symbolic funeral or purification rite, but given Anna's elevated status, it's more for external show." Ma paused again and tentatively added, "James would like us to film the ceremony."

Maggie shook her head. "Take still photos, but a film will get onto YouTube, and create too much notoriety." She paused, then added, "And please make an announcement of such for those with cell phone cameras."

Ma stared at Maggie for a long moment. "As you wish, but this will not be a sannyasa, or *mantra diksha*, initiation. Swami Vinanda agrees with me that Anna is fully self-realized, and should bear the name Sri Annananda Ma, and as such is required to give her 'blessing' at the end of the ceremony—all of which will be hard to contain."

"Especially if she heals everybody present," Maggie said with mild irritation.

Ma began to reply, but Anna added, "I not control energy. I give it out, and it does what it does."

Maggie nodded her head. "And this will happen tomorrow?"

"No. We want to give you a day of rest and thoroughly go over the ceremony with the two of you."

"And allow time for the word to get out," Maggie added.

Ma smiled indulgently. "This is a joyous occasion, my dear."

"Yes, of course."

Anna slipped off Guru's lap and stepped down to sit next to her mother, but Maggie beat her to the punch line. "I know, 'Don't worry, be happy.'"

Anna smiled and patted her mother on the arm for reassurance.

That night Maggie dreamed that her daughter was sitting on a park bench, and then the clouds parted and a stream of intense bright light shown on her, filled with circling doves. She woke up and patted Anna on the head. It all seemed to be decreed from on high, and she just needed to go with the flow.

After morning tea, Prema came for them and they were taken to the temple room. Ma had written out, even before they arrived yesterday, the ceremony's format and handed Maggie a copy for her to read. Since only a swami could initiate one into the dasanami order with its lineage, Ma would conduct the ceremony but would be aided by several esteemed swamis and swaminis from ashrams up and down the West Coast.

"Did you send out an alert?" Maggie asked.

"No, but as I said, the yogi grapevine was abuzz, and I've gotten several calls this week from spiritual adepts, and it only adds to the authenticity of the ceremony for one so young."

Maggie nodded her head, but if these swamis heard about it, she could imagine their devotees swarming the ashram ceremony. She posed that question to Ma.

Ma replied, "I told them they could come, but only my ashram devotees were allowed inside the compound for the ceremony, including James Edwards and Marsha Singh."

"Thank you."

"The first order will be my asking Anna if she has gotten permission from her mother to enter the order."

Anna looked up at her mother. "Do I, Mama?"

Maggie nodded her head. "Yes, but you can't leave home and join the yogi circus."

Anna and Ma laughed, and this lightened the mood. "Yes," Ma added, "but the question still needs to be part of the ceremony."

Maggie said, "I'll leave out the circus bit."

Ma smiled. "Next will be the agreed upon external and internal renunciations, or *tyaga* and *vairagya*. I know Anna is a little young to consider renouncing worldly pleasures and positions and her attachment to them—"

"No. I not too young. I do not wish pleasures or positions, money or...fame."

Ma looked agape at Anna. "My dear, these are the three *eshanas* that are usually renounced. Is this ceremony not new to you?"

"No, Ma. I...initiate you and Mama in other lives."

Ma let out a deep sigh and turned to Maggie. "This ceremony is going to be quite monumental."

The swamis and swaminis started to arrive later that afternoon. Prema was sent to gather Anna and Maggie for introductions, prior to the evening meal. Anna was installed on the pillow next to Ma on her dais and greeted the holy men and women who had come for her initiatory ceremony. Some stood, others sat cross-legged on pillows, but all engaged Anna curious as to the legitimacy of Ma hi' Ma's claims of her self-realized status. Anna answered all their inquiries with spiritually astute replies if in a childlike manner, and after a while they all bowed to the Spirit alive in young Anna Jane Langford. Maggie stood back and listened to her daughter and knew that the true nature of her being could not be contained now, and despite pledges to honor her right to privacy as a child, that the world would soon know of her and beat a path to their door. Maggie wondered if moving to India was not indeed a better option.

That night, after an elaborate dinner where Anna sat with Ma at the head of the table, they retired to their quarters. After Anna's bath, Maggie tucked her into their bed, but before she could leave, Anna grabbed her hand. "I know you're afraid of people knowing of me, but as you say, maybe why I was born here."

"Yes, dear. That makes sense, but despite the many Hindu and Buddhist practitioners in America, this is still a Christian country, and it will be difficult for them to understand, not less accept you for who you are."

Anna smiled in the dim light. "Who I am is who they are in inner being, and maybe time for…wake-up call."

Maggie could only bow her head. "Maybe."

The *bibidisa* ceremony the next morning was sacred and overwhelming as Anna's energy seemed to magnify the heightened energies of all the swamis and swaminis present. Some devotees passed out and needed to be attended to, others cried as the fire purification ceremony further purified and released the remaining dross matter of their own being. All bowed, as the flower-draped child swamini gave her blessing:

"I am moved by ceremony to honor God in me and God in you, and the blessing I give is not of me but of the Spirit that moves through all beings—the eye of the eye, the ear of the ear, the mind of the mind, the life of life. Always honor and all will be right with you."

Anna waved her hand, and many in the audience could feel her healing energy permeate their being, and for some it relieved them of their lingering afflictions.

As the swamis and swaminis walked away from the ceremony, all were moved by the energy of young Anna and her message, and a few asked Ma and then Maggie if they had ever read her *The Kena Upanishad* that Anna had quoted in her blessing. While she had a copy of *The Upanishads* on her bookshelf, Maggie said she had not yet read any of it to her daughter. They nodded their heads realizing that this child was indeed a master from centuries past, and no doubt drew on an earlier understanding of this most sacred text.

Maggie and Anna stayed one more day to let the energy of her initiation settle, but they needed to pick Bodhi up the next day from James Edwards's dog sitter and didn't want to burden her any further, although she would assure Maggie that it was a delight to keep him. But this extra day allowed Maggie and Ma to have further discussions with James and Dr. Singh, who stayed on after Sunday's ceremony and which had only infused their resolve to protect the unfoldment of Sri Annananda Ma.

Chapter 31

Several days after they returned from the ashram, Maggie received a certified letter in the mail from the superintendent of the San Luis Obispo County Office of Education. She was informed that her August 15 meeting with Mrs. Linden had been moved to his offices on Education Drive off Highway 1 northwest of the city to accommodate some school board members, and would be presided over by the Superintendent Gerald Henderson. She went out and faxed a copy to James Edwards. He called later in the day to reassure her that he had expected as much, and again suggested that he bring Dr. Singh with him to the meeting. Maggie didn't want them tromping into the meeting with a whole entourage of people and taking a defensive posture. The simpler they made it, the better for her and Anna. But, Maggie did call a local child psychologist, who agreed to administer an IQ test for Anna and give her the results the same day.

Maggie was also alerted to the spliced-together video of still photos of Anna's swamini's initiation that appeared on YouTube. She called James, but he told her that it was almost impossible to get this website to take down posted videos, citing freedom of the press statutes. Anna and her mother watched it so they would at least be prepared to address any questions directed at them from its presentation. As expected, the psychologist certified her IQ at around 140. Maggie added the certificate to her folder of information that she would bring to the meeting with the superintendent and the school board.

James Edwards flew into town the night before the meeting. He was staying at the Granada Hotel & Bistro, and they drove into town to eat dinner with him. James met them in the lobby and they looked over the bistro's menu, which wasn't to their liking so they walked to the Big Sky Café with its Western décor and paintings and more varied menu. He ordered the crab cakes, and Maggie and Anna shared the grilled eggplant dish. While they were waiting for their meals and drinking iced tea, James asked Maggie how she felt about tomorrow's meeting.

"Well, I'm a bit apprehensive, but this is San Luis Obispo, not Cleveland," she said, remembering having made this reference at some point earlier.

"I've talked to a colleague in Santa Barbara, who had lived here for a while and had children in the school system, and he said that Superintendent Henderson, who replaced the guy who bamboozled you when you were pregnant, has a good reputation for being fair and aboveboard and was open to alternative spirituality. However, there were members on the county board of education who were, to quote him, 'a bunch of sticks-in-the-mud.'"

Anna smiled at this description. "We stir the pool?"

Maggie looked over at her daughter. "We will answer their questions as best we can, and not hide anything from them."

James looked at Maggie. "You're going to let Anna speak for herself?"

She nodded her head. "Swamini Annananda says it's 'about her,' so she wants them to ask her their questions."

"This could be interesting."

Maggie smiled. "They're in for a big surprise if they think they can railroad my Anna."

James laughed. "I would think."

The next morning Maggie and Anna drove to the County Office of Education building outside town in a modern white-adobe Spanish-styled building with wood pilasters and a garden of desert plants and Saguaro cactus. They waited in the lobby until James arrived, and they were then ushered into a conference room where several men and women were seated, including a stern-looking Mrs. Linden, and they sat across the table from them.

"I'd like to welcome the three of you, and especially young

Anna, to this meeting. I'm Gerald Henderson, the county superintendent of education."

He was a man of medium height with dark hair, a good build, and kind if observant eyes. Maggie wondered if he was a meditator.

"We are glad to meet you," Anna volunteered.

"Thank you, Anna. But first let me address some questions to your mother and her lawyer..." He looked down at his folder. "James Edwards, who..."

"Who represents the devotees of Hindu Guru Ma hi' Ma," James added.

Henderson nodded his head. "But, this meeting is about education, not religious freedom of expression."

"Well, I'm here to make sure that's what it's about."

"I see."

Henderson turned to Maggie. "Ms. Langdon, for the last two years you have been homeschooling your daughter Anna, and this past year had three East Indian Hindu children in the first grade?"

"Yes, that is correct."

"I see that Mr. Edwards has filed forms to turn your homeschooling venue into a religious school, but your degrees are in secondary education, and arts and craft."

"I believe you'll find in the submitted papers," James added, "a document by Guru Ma hi' Ma that certifies Ms. Langdon as a teacher of Hindu religion."

A board member, Ms. Beverly Holmes, spoke up. "Which in our opinion she is unqualified to certify. We would prefer, as in our other religious schools, a degree in Hindu studies from a recognized university or college."

"You not teach mind to be holy, you bring out spirit," Anna added.

Henderson smiled and turned to Edwards and said rather evenhandedly. "I consider this religious school affiliation as a maneuver to protect young Anna's spiritual expression and not have that or her classified as...afflicted."

James was about to object, but Henderson put up his hand. "Sir, the county's head school psychologist, Dr. Adam Schultz, has reviewed Dr. Singh's testing of young Anna's emotional stability and test scores for her rather high IQ." Henderson turned to look down the row of board members to a middle-aged man with short blond hair and stylish blue-tinted glasses who held up his hand. "He knows the good doctor and we accept her testing results, so this is not an issue."

"Very well," Edwards said, as Maggie sighed in relief.

He turned to Anna. "I see Anna where you were recently initiated as a Hindu Swami. The YouTube video of the ceremony was quite moving, as was your recorded blessing."

"I Swamini."

"Yes, of course, let's not be gender-biased." This drew a few chuckles from his colleagues. "I also have read about your healings recently in India. Tell me about that."

James was about to object, but Anna raised her hand and he stopped himself. Henderson and the others noted that and looked at each other.

"There was an old yogi in clinic with..."

"Early-stage pancreatic cancer," Maggie added.

"He suffer much. I ask his spirit, and it say he ready to be healed. So I heal him."

"You'll find his ashram doctor's report of the yogi's cancer remission in your folder," James said.

"Yes, Mr. Edwards. You've been quite thorough in making your case, but let's let Anna make hers." He turned to Anna. "How does that work, Anna?"

"I...energize connection with his spirit, and it heals the body."

"I see, and where do you get the energy to do this?"

"Not my energy, God's energy, works through me."

Another one of the board members added, "Faith healings

hardly ever pan out."

Anna looked at her and said, "You come to my house, and I heal liver, and we see."

The woman gawked at her, before tears arose in her eyes.

Another board member turned to James Edwards. "The girl has been prepped very thoroughly by Mr. Edwards, but—"

Anna interrupted him. "Sorry, but I not need anybody to speak for me."

Henderson smiled. "I can see that, Swamini." He looked down at his open folder and turned to Maggie. "I have a complaint here registered from a Mr. Kumar whose son was being taught by you that, to quote him, 'Anna teleported the class to an... astral park to meet with Anna's guide, Joseph.'"

Maggie was about to answer him, but again Anna raised her hand. "I not take the body. I shift spirit, like in dream state."

Edwards added, before he was stood down by his young client, "This is an advanced spiritual practice, but not beyond the scope of Indian yogis."

"As your book excerpts document, Mr. Edwards," Henderson said wearily, "but the question here is how a seven-year-old American girl can do such a thing."

Edwards was about to reply when Anna smiled at him and he desisted. She turned back to the superintendent.

"When I was born, I open my eyes and see mother and other women and spirit people and know that I born awake. I not can tell anybody until later, but I not lose connection to spirit, like others do, so that is how I move energy."

Henderson sat back in his chair and raised his own hand to quiet the other board members who were ready to jump into the fray. "Anna, that is a most remarkable statement, but the question here..." He turned to both Maggie and James Edwards. "Is Anna's effect on the children who are homeschooled, or attend this religious school, with her." He raised a hand to stop James Edwards before he could make another reference. "Yes, I have read the affidavits from the parents of the others students, but like Mr. Kumar's son Amir, some yet to enroll here may not be ready for such…advanced spiritual practices."

Anna volunteered, "Yes, I now know. I talk with Joseph; he tell me I need allow others develop on own, that my energy will affect them and they use as needed."

Henderson nodded his head. "This is the most…unusual educational situation I've ever heard of, but looking at young Anna, or as I too can now say, Swamini Annananda, and listening to her, I have no doubt of the authenticity of the claims made of her. But…" he turned to James Edwards, "I will insist that a more thorough registration statement be made of what children who enter this school will encounter learning beside Swamini, to be signed by their parents and that I will take more seriously any further…demonstrations such as Mr. Kumar objected to."

"Agreed. I will draw it up for your approval," Edwards said with great relief.

"Gerald, I think this whole situation requires more study," Beverly Holmes added.

"Good, I'll appoint you, Beverly, as their school monitor, and you can periodically check with Ms. Langford and the parents of her students as to her upholding of our agreement."

Henderson turned to Maggie. "When Anna gets older, have you thought of creating a healing center here in San Luis Obispo? Or have her affiliated with the Banyan Tree Center?"

Maggie smiled. "No, not really, but we'll see how Swamini develops and how her *Lila*, or divine impulse, moves her."

"Okay, I understand that." Henderson turned to the board members, then back to the three of them. "This issue has been resolved to my satisfaction and this meeting is adjourned." Maggie, Anna, and James Edwards stood up and headed for the door, while the board members gathered around Superintendent Henderson, some to voice their objections. As they stepped out of the room, they could hear him say, "The mayor would like us

to have our own...Krishnamurti, like what transpired in Ojai."
This last statement gave Maggie pause for thought.

Chapter 32

With the Krishna Hindu School officially certified, Maggie accepted two new students for the second grade in September, along with Gish and Debby, who had reverted back to her Hindu name of Devi, much to her parents' delight. They were Jema, whose father operated a jewelry store that specialized in East Indian stones, and Piku, whose father taught physics at the local high school, but wanted his son to be educated, or at least for now, in an ashram school as he referred to it. He had told Maggie on their initial interview that "I don't want my son to turn out like these Western heathens I teach." Neither parent was surprised by the registration form nor its disclaimer that they were required to sign. They had heard rumors from those in their Hindu community about the child guru, and after meeting Anna were both enthusiastic about her influence on their children's spiritual development. Jema's father added with smile, "Well, at least I won't have to get health insurance." Maggie tried to persuade him otherwise, and he laughed and said of course his son was covered under their family policy.

But, as Maggie had feared, people began to call, email her, and some even showed up at their door wanting healings from the "child saint." She consented for children with life-threatening illnesses, after Anna contacted and received permission from their spirit, which did not always happen, much to their parents' distress and further entreaty. Finally Gary, with Maggie's consent, built an eight-foot-tall pinewood fence around his property with a yard and garage door on a remote locking system and with an embedded speaker box and a topside camera at the front gate. Patrol cars, at the mayor's insistence, made daily drive-bys and cleared the street when necessary of those waiting for healings or *darsana seekers* looking for a glimpse of the child saint, which in Hindu lore bestowed its own blessing. After three months the commotion surrounding Anna died down somewhat, but it was difficult for them to freely move about town without being accosted by the sick or religiously afflicted, as Gary called them. Anna took their isolation easier than Maggie, but at least once a month, she would drive them down to Santa Barbara to visit her parents just to step out on the street or walk the beach unmolested.

Maggie was thinking of staying home for Christmas, but that was before Anna's elaborate eighth-birthday celebration at Agam and Jade Chandra's estate, where the invited guests were warned against seeking healings or bringing birthday gifts, but all of them showed up with the traditional flower leis that were draped over both her and her child. In the end Anna spontaneously gave the gathering her "birthday" blessing, which extended the party until most could recover from their dazed state to drive their families home. When Maggie and Anna returned home, they found mounds of flower bouquets lining the fence outside their home, with more being delivered by local florist trucks every hour. Anna insisted that they walk down the row and read all the inscribed notes. While most were from local Hindus and Ma devotees, there were some from other states and countries. Anna stopped and read one from Mother Meera with her small colored oval photo. This modern Hindu saint, who now lived in Germany and who had had her first samadhi experience at age six, wanted Maggie to contact her about Sri Annananda Ma.

Anna looked up at her mother. "I see her face in my meditations. We go to visit her?"

"I hear she comes to America on tours."

Anna nodded her head and continued walking down the row, as Maggie collected the notes to respond to those with land or email addresses.

Her daughter's increasing spiritual notoriety was what Maggie had feared most about the circumstances surrounding the school board's summons and the precautions they had taken, especially Anna's swamini initiation and its subsequent YouTube exposure. But, what really alarmed her was Hari Kumar's "letter to the editor" that appeared in *The Tribune* that week, telling about his son Amir being taken to an astral park while studying with the so-called child saint, and that she was a threat to the community. "I mean, what would prevent her from taking the President to this park and leaving him there." This brought an outpouring of disclaimers from local residents, many of whom claimed that Hari and Amir had watched too many *Avengers* and *X-Men* movies, and a spiritually informed reply that Anna transported the boy's spirit not his body. What seemed to settle the matter was an editorial op by Superintendent Henderson who said that the school board had met with Anna and her mother about Mr. Kumar's complaint, which was somewhat exaggerated, and were satisfied by Sri Annananda's promise to avoid such demonstrations in the future, which did not discount what had happened.

Maggie needed to get her and Anna out of town, and so she started the school's Christmas break a week early, which would extend until after the New Year. The children were delighted and their parents, who had no doubt been following the brouhaha over Anna and her powers, acquiesced. So Maggie alerted her parents to their change of plans and her wish for an extended stay, packed up Anna and Bodhi, and they headed down to Santa Barbara two days later. Maggie's sister Jill, who had heard from Grace about the controversy and the initiation of her niece Anna as a Hindu swamini, was appalled by "her sister's reckless disregard for her child's welfare." Her family had planned on coming home for Christmas, but withdrew saying she didn't want to expose her child to this kind of religious hysteria.

After their arrival, and while Anna was taking her nap and Bodhi was being walked by her father, Maggie sat down on the patio with her mother for tea and to read Jill's scathing emails.

She could only shake her head.

"She's always felt threatened by my Eastern spirituality and Anna's blossoming has really pushed her over the edge."

"Well dear, in all fairness, this is a lot to take in," Grace added, while taking hold of her daughter's hand.

Maggie laughed. "Tell me about it."

"Your father is concerned about your welfare. There are a lot of religiously unhinged people out there." Grace paused and looked Maggie in the eyes. "Do you feel safe there?"

"The mayor is a supporter of ours, and patrol cars drive by daily, and Anna does have a guard dog."

Grace shook her head. "Who can be bought off by treats." Maggie smiled. "Maybe you should consider moving back with us."

Maggie laughed. "That would really drive Dad crazy, not to mention me." She squeezed her mother's hand. "We'll be all right. I've heard from Thomas, who has apparently been updated on his daughter's...situation, and said he might move back to America sooner."

"Well that's good to hear."

"And, of all things, our next door neighbor, Bill Stevens, stopped by. Said he was a retired Navy SEAL, gave us his number, and said to call anytime we feel threatened or even pestered."

Grace smiled. "Is he single?" Maggie rolled her eyes.

A few days later, Grace, Maggie and Anna went Christmas shopping at the Paseo Nuevo mall on the eastside of town. While Maggie shopped for gifts, Grace and Anna sat at an outdoor café sipping hot chocolates. Suddenly Anna put down her cup, closed her eyes, and then turned her head as she watched young Amir Kumar approach their table.

"Hi, Amir," Anna said openheartedly.

Kumar stopped a few feet away and just glared at Anna.

Grace said, "Anna, do you know this boy?"

"Grandma, this is Amir, who used to be in our school." Grace immediately made the connection to the boy and his father. She took out her cell phone and called her daughter.

"I found my own Joseph," he spit out, "and he not like you. Promises to give me...powers."

Anna squinted her eyes and could see the dark aura around Amir, and the cord to an even darker force in another realm.

"Amir," Anna said with all the kindness she could muster, "love for others and self, not hate, is the way to such...powers."

The angry little boy just shook his head. "We see."

Maggie arrived on the scene. "Amir. What are you doing here?"

The boy smiled, as the darkness around him evaporated. "We're visiting friends and Christmas shopping."

Amir's mother, Paramita, hurried over. "There you are." She looked at the alarmed expression on the women's faces. "What did you say to them?"

Amir just shrugged his shoulder. Anna looked up at her. "Hi, Mrs. Kumar. Amir in trouble. Need to clear his aura and break cords."

Amir glared back at Anna with daggers in his eyes.

Paramita just shook her head and turned to Maggie. "I'm so sorry if he said anything inappropriate. I'll have a talk with him."

"Paramita, please keep your son away from my daughter," Maggie said, surprised by her own rudeness.

Without saying another word, Paramita dragged her son away.

"Maggie," her mother added after a moment. "That little boy is mentally unbalanced. You need to report him."

Anna shook her head and interrupted them. "Light and dark play together. You see, Mama."

Grace agreed not to mention this encounter to Mark, and the rest of their stay was peaceful, although several of her neighbors inquired about Anna's availability to treat them. Grace told them in no uncertain terms to go to their doctor.

One bright spot was when they went for a walk on the beach with Bodhi. A man in a white suit and panama hat walked past them, and said with an Indian accent, "Don't worry, be happy." Maggie looked at him as he turned his head and she saw the characteristic hooked nose and bushy black mustache of Meher Baba.

"He look after us too," Anna said, as Maggie glanced down at her daughter. When she looked up, the man or apparition had disappeared.

Maggie didn't tell her parents this story; her father was already up in arms about "all this Indian guru malarkey." But it was reassuring to her, and because of this lovely spirit manifestation, she was better prepared to return them to their life in San Luis Obispo, but could only wonder what the future would bring and how they would handle Anna's new spiritual notoriety.

Acknowledgments

Spiritual or visionary fiction has always been a difficult genre for publishers, but I would like to acknowledge the pioneering work done in this genre by Robert Friedman and Frank DeMarco at Hampton Roads Publishing starting in the 1990s and continuing for years. They always felt that storytelling was a powerful tool for presenting cutting-edge ideas, be they metaphysical or speculative. I can still remember meeting with Bob forty years ago and passing him the manuscript for my first novel, *Starborn*, my little mystical tale, which he hoped would be another *Jonathan Livingston Seagull*. Its sales didn't quite meet those high expectations, but I wrote two more visionary fiction titles for him, the last of which *Matrix of the Gods* Frank edited. In today's marketplace, this genre is even a harder sell, but I appreciate that John Hunt continues to publish spiritual, visionary, and speculative fiction under his varied imprints. I can only hope that his faith in this genre will be rewarded someday.

About the Author

John Nelson is the author of the novels *Starborn, Transformations,* and *Matrix of the Gods,* originally published by Hampton Roads Publishing, and *I, Human* published by Cosmic Egg. He authored the nonfiction book *The Magic Mirror,* which won the 2008 COVR Award as best book of the year and best divination system, and more recently *A Guide of Energetic Healing.*

Nelson was the editorial director of Bear & Company in the mid-1990s and Inner Ocean Publishing in the early 2000s. He is the owner of Bookworks Ltd., where he edits fiction and nonfiction books for a variety of authors and publishers. This includes *The Sacred Promise* by Gary Schwartz, *The White House Doctor* by Dr. Connie Mariano, *The 12-Step Buddhist, Yoga and the Twelve-Step Path, The Buddha Speaks, Bright Light* by Dee Wallace, and the YA novel *Avatar Magic.*

Nelson has been a yogi and a meditator for fifty years and brings an expanded consciousness perspective to all that he writes. His fiction is usually a blend of hard science, science fiction, and psycho-spiritual insights, but *The Miracle of Anna* is strictly spiritual or visionary fiction. Nelson's two nonfiction works are based on his own personal spiritual explorations. Visit his website at www.johnnelsonbookworks.com.

Roundfire

FICTION

Put simply, we publish great stories. Whether it's literary or popular, a gentle tale or a pulsating thriller, the connecting theme in all Roundfire fiction titles is that once you pick them up you won't want to put them down.
If you have enjoyed this book, why not tell other readers by posting a review on your preferred book site.

Recent bestsellers from Roundfire are:

The Bookseller's Sonnets
Andi Rosenthal
The Bookseller's Sonnets intertwines three love stories with a tale
of religious identity and mystery spanning five hundred years
and three countries.
Paperback: 978-1-84694-342-3 ebook: 978-184694-626-4

Birds of the Nile
An Egyptian Adventure
N.E. David
Ex-diplomat Michael Blake wanted a quiet birding trip up the
Nile – he wasn't expecting a revolution.
Paperback: 978-1-78279-158-4 ebook: 978-1-78279-157-7

Blood Profit$
The Lithium Conspiracy
J. Victor Tomaszek, James N. Patrick, Sr.
The blood of the many for the profits of the few... *Blood Profit$*
will take you into the cigar-smoke-filled room where American
policy and laws are really made.
Paperback: 978-1-78279-483-7 ebook: 978-1-78279-277-2

The Burden
A Family Saga
N.E. David
Frank will do anything to keep his mother and father apart. But
he's carrying baggage – and it might just weigh him down ...
Paperback: 978-1-78279-936-8 ebook: 978-1-78279-937-5

The Cause
Roderick Vincent
The second American Revolution will be a fire lit from an internal spark.
Paperback: 978-1-78279-763-0 ebook: 978-1-78279-762-3

Don't Drink and Fly
The Story of Bernice O'Hanlon: Part One
Cathie Devitt
Bernice is a witch living in Glasgow. She loses her way in her life and wanders off the beaten track looking for the garden of enlightenment.
Paperback: 978-1-78279-016-7 ebook: 978-1-78279-015-0

Gag
Melissa Unger
One rainy afternoon in a Brooklyn diner, Peter Howland punctures an egg with his fork. Repulsed, Peter pushes the plate away and never eats again.
Paperback: 978-1-78279-564-3 ebook: 978-1-78279-563-6

The Master Yeshua
The Undiscovered Gospel of Joseph
Joyce Luck
Jesus is not who you think he is. The year is 75 CE. Joseph ben Jude is frail and ailing, but he has a prophecy to fulfil …
Paperback: 978-1-78279-974-0 ebook: 978-1-78279-975-7

Tuareg
Alberto Vazquez-Figueroa
With over 5 million copies sold worldwide, *Tuareg* is a classic adventure story from best-selling author Alberto Vazquez-Figueroa, about honour, revenge and a clash of cultures.
Paperback: 978-1-84694-192-4

On the Far Side, There's a Boy
Paula Coston
Martine Haslett, a thirty-something 1980s woman, plays hard
on the fringes of the London drag club scene until one night
which prompts her to sign up to a charity. She writes to a
young Sri Lankan boy, with consequences far and long.
Paperback: 978-1-78279-574-2 ebook: 978-1-78279-573-5

Readers of ebooks can buy or view any of these bestsellers by
clicking on the live link in the title. Most titles are published
in paperback and as an ebook. Paperbacks are available in
traditional bookshops. Both print and ebook formats are
available online.

Find more titles and sign up to our readers' newsletter at
http://www.johnhuntpublishing.com/fiction

Follow us on Facebook at
https://www.facebook.com/JHPfiction
and Twitter at https://twitter.com/JHPFiction